4TH SILENCE

SCHOCK SISTERS MYSTERY SERIES
BOOK 4

MISTY EVANS

ADRIENNE GIORDANO

ALG PUBLISHING, LLC

1

Charlie

The ghosts of the dead haunt me night and day. They don't take vacations or holidays.

As I pull into the icy parking lot behind Schock Investigations—the business I run with my sister, Meg—my phone dings with a message from my mother. Helen Schock doesn't take vacations or holidays, either.

Snow falls thick and heavy on my windshield. While the lot has been plowed by the service the building owner employs, the asphalt is disappearing under the phantom white flakes at such a speed that it'll need another pass within the hour. Meg's battered minivan sits under at least two inches of the wet stuff, telling me she's been here for hours.

She doesn't sleep much, my sister. The ghosts haunt her, too.

My fingers are stiff from the cold as I tug off my gloves, shut off my Christmas playlist, and read the message. *I made the news!* A video is attached.

My mother is as obsessed with bringing closure to victims and their families as Meg and I. It's probably where we got our love for the hunt. Maybe 'love' is the wrong term. This passion for our work is all-consuming.

The psychologist in me knows 'passion' isn't accurate either, at least not for my mother and sister. They are obsessed. Fixated. Addicted, even. Solving cold cases is a compulsion for them.

For me, it's more about vengeance, plain and simple. Justice. If I let myself go down the emotional rabbit holes they do concerning the victims, I'd never get out of bed. To hold on to my sanity, I fixate on the killers instead. I profile them, find their triggers, and track them down.

My view of the back entrance to the building vanishes as the snow blankets the windshield. My thumb hovers over the video. I should check on Meg first. Make coffee if she hasn't already done so. I'm doing what I can to cut costs, and buying my usual cup of wake-up-and-act-like-a-human-being latte on the way to work isn't in the budget this month. With Christmas comes bonuses and raises for our meager staff. While I can afford the peppermint latte from the place down the street, every dollar I save takes pressure off me to keep the business afloat.

Helen Schock, however, is a handful. If I don't respond in the next five-point-oh seconds, she'll call. If I don't answer that, she'll show up here, D.C. snowstorm be damned.

Haley, our receptionist, texted earlier to tell me she'll be late —her car is dead. Matt Stephens, our part-time investigator, is stopping by her place to give her battery a jump. Neither of them will be here to run interference if Mom shows up, and I'll have to delay our required Monday morning meeting.

I've got to nip the Helen Schock apocalypse in the bud.

First, coffee. *Driving*, I text back. *Will watch when I get to the office.* I pray it's enough to satisfy her for five minutes.

Inside, I flip on the lights, remove my coat, and shake wet droplets of melting snow from my hair. "Meg?" I call.

No answer.

We closed a case over the weekend, thanks to her diligence in reconstructing a skull, along with an unexpected lead I uncovered. One of her 'girls in the basement' now has a name —Galishea Tern.

JJ Carrington, the U.S. Attorney for the District of Columbia, is contacting Galishea's family today. Her remains will be home for Christmas. Her family will find some closure, and JJ, the Emperor of Cold Cases, has a killer to nail.

That means Meg is onto another case. The next John or Jane Doe. The next girl in the basement. Although we close numerous missing persons and cold cases, her collection of lost souls continues to grow. As does her obsession with it.

When it comes to my family, being a psychologist and former FBI profiler sucks. I know what's 'clinically' wrong with each and every one of us. And I can't do a damn thing about it.

I wipe dirty sludge from my black leather boots and slip into the small kitchenette that doubles as our lunchroom. No surprise, my sister hasn't made coffee. Yesterday's leftover dregs, the same color as the sludge, have stained the inside of the pot. I go to work to clean it and start a fresh pot.

How long has she been here, obsessing over her reconstructed skulls that still have no identities?

While the coffee brews, I consider whether I'll need to shovel the sidewalk. Our landlord has the service plow the lot, but we're responsible for clearing the walkways ourselves. I glance at my three-inch-heeled boots, more of a fashion statement than a practical winter choice. Matt can do it. A former police officer, Matt "Mad Dog" Stephens, has more muscles than The Rock and likes to show them off. He's also got a classic "save the damsel in distress" personality. On a day like today, I'm not above putting both of those traits to good use.

I text him, but I get no reply. He's probably driving or already at Haley's, monkeying with her car. A second message from my mother comes in: *I'm on my way.*

What? Cursing, I hurriedly type back, *Why?*

If you'd watch the clip I sent, you'd know.

Sighing, I tap the screen. The sound of "Silent Night" issues from my phone's speaker, and a reporter from Channel 4 News stands in front of an iron gate surrounding a majestic, historic home from the early twentieth century. "This is Denise Brown. I'm here in Wesley Heights tonight at the Hartman family home where eight-year-old Tiffany Ashley Rugers-Hartman was brutally murdered thirty years ago on Christmas Eve."

The Silent Night Murder. I lean against the cabinet and sigh again, rubbing my temple. One headache coming up. Of course, my investigative reporter mother would champion the revival of this old case.

The camera pans out to the three-story brick home behind the tall gates, conservatively decorated for the season, as a group bundled in coats and scarves sings the carol in soft voices. A memorial has been created on the lawn with candles, teddy bears, and Christmas wreaths. Folks have tied cards and handmade signs to the iron gates.

A school picture of the girl appears on the screen. Her smile shows a missing tooth. I swallow hard.

Denise Brown's voice continues over the photo. "On this anniversary of Tiffany's death, many in the community are asking law enforcement to reopen the case to expose the killer and finally find justice for the poor little girl."

Next, she interviews my mother. Helen Schock, her natural silver-streaked hair tucked under a knit cap, stares down the camera with eyes that could cut glass. As lead investigator for the Crime Desk of the D.C. Investigative Journal—a tabloid that keeps the local cold case hunters stirred up—Mom's breath frosts the air, and her eyes snap with determination. Brown introduces her to the viewers, then asks about the Silent Night case and why she and the others are holding a vigil outside the family's home.

"What happened to that little girl is unacceptable." Her tone is no-nonsense. I heard it routinely during my childhood. Still do today. "She didn't even get to wake up on Christmas morning with her family. Can you imagine dying so young? Not just dying—she was killed! On Christmas Eve, surrounded by family and friends." She blinks away tears. "I've learned that there is new DNA evidence and details about that party that law enforcement refuses to reexamine. Someone who attended it knows what happened." She glares into the camera, pointing a finger at the viewers. "Citizens Solving Cold Cases will solve this case once and for all."

I cringe. JJ will be calling before I can finish my coffee, insisting I rein her in.

Mom started Citizens Solving Cold Cases a few years ago. It went defunct, but she's revived it. She's relentless about recruiting new members and utilizing them to delve into the thousands of unsolved cases in the D.C. area.

I wish her luck.

Stewing, I pour two cups of coffee and retrieve a couple protein bars from my bag. This will take patience and damage control. Patience with my mother, damage control with JJ. Is Mom correct, though? Is there new DNA evidence? Has the family asked to reopen the case based on it? Has JJ and his team refused?

At the door of Meg's office, the video and questions take a back seat. My sister sits in the middle of the floor, files scattered around her, two of her sketchbooks open and filled with drawings and notes. "The answer is here," she says without preamble. "I have to find it."

Stepping past a stack, I hand her the coffee and one of the bars. "Who are you zeroed in on now?"

"Darcy." She sets my offerings aside. "Her remains were found two miles from Galishea's. The time of death places them within a few months of each other. Could be the same killer."

"I'll help you go through the files after the meeting." I don't have time to do it, but I'll make it at some point today. I have the Costnick trial across town this afternoon. The defense has hired me as an expert witness for their client, and I'll have to leave early to ensure I arrive promptly.

"What meeting?" Meg asks without looking up.

"It's Monday."

Her gaze meets mine, eyes glassy from lack of sleep. "So?"

"Our Monday morning meeting, Meg?"

The lightbulb goes off, and she releases a pent-up huff that blows a piece of her hair back from her forehead. "Sorry. I just got..."

The words trail off, as does her attention.

"Did you sleep at all last night?"

She takes a sip and shakes her head. "I can't."

"Why don't you take some of those gummy bears Jerome has? Won't they put you to sleep?"

Her boyfriend deals weed, but he has a legit medical card now, too. She snorts. "He's the problem."

My hackles rise automatically. If he's done something to upset her... "How so?"

She presses her lips together. Her focus drifts to the chaotic piles on the floor, then to the bold collection of paintings on her walls. "He asked me to"—her hand shakes enough to spill the coffee, and she jumps up, dripping hot liquid onto her skirt and the sketchbooks—"do something ridiculous."

I take the cup so she can grab a napkin and wipe the liquid off the files. My mind churns with various scenarios. "Ridiculous, how? Like, kinky ridiculous?"

"He didn't so much ask me as just...hinted at it."

"The suspense is killing me. Spit it out."

She brushes past me, heading for the kitchen. The office landline out front begins to ring. As I follow, she says over her shoulder, "Should you get that?"

I ignore her attempt to distract me. "Meg." Jeez, I sound like Mom.

She grabs a dish towel from the counter and wets a corner before dabbing at her skirt. "It's nothing. Forget I said anything."

The phone continues blaring at Haley's desk. "Tell me before Mom gets here."

She pauses in her ministrations. "Mom's coming?"

"She's revived the Silent Night murder case with her club."

Meg processes this. "I saw her on the news last night. It's good she's bringing light to it again. We should help."

I don't disagree. I just can't imagine how I'll allocate resources to it. We run on a shoestring budget. There's no payoff in this kind of investigation—the reward the family offered thirty years ago is no longer available. Unless they were to hire us to look into it, it's a freebie.

I'm not heartless, but those don't pay the bills. We won't be able to help anyone if we go bankrupt.

Meg reads my mind. "You know we have to do this. Help Tiffany. If we solve the case, it will make the news. We'll get more paying clients from it."

The dead plague me. I haven't been right since my first cold case at the Bureau. It's still unsolved.

My sister's pleading, bloodshot eyes weigh on me. I set both cups on the counter, anticipating ringing Jerome's neck. "What did Jerome ask you to do?"

She starts to reply, but the back door flies open, and our mother rushes in like the blizzard raging outside, bringing a gust of snow and cold with her. "I'm here!" She whips past the kitchen door with stacks of file boxes on a wheeled cart. She sees us out of the corner of her eye and backpedals, blustering into the kitchen and filling it with her energy.

Her face is flushed. The ringing phone stops and starts again. "I've gone viral on TikTok." Pride laces her voice. "I used your number for people to call with any information on the case." She dumps a box into my arms, pushes her hood back, and removes her gloves, grinning like it's the best day ever. "Pour me some coffee, Meg." Her gaze tracks to me. "We've got a lot of work to do."

2

Meg

"**Y**ou gave out our office number?" Charlie asks in that quiet, steady tone that means death to all.

Our mother—the woman who can't resist a cold case—sails past, wheeling her cart stacked high with boxes behind her.

"Of course," she says, as if Charlie is the irrational one for even asking. "I couldn't exactly use my cell. Your father would kill me."

"I might kill you."

On cue, the phone rings, the repetitive noise blaring from the receptionist's desk and the conference room. I sometimes have nightmares about that sound. It's why I tend to work with earbuds in. The bleeping drives me half mad and now pulls me from the oncoming storm between the two women I love most.

I fall in step behind Mom and give Charlie the here-we-go look.

In the conference room, I glance at the device sitting on the credenza. Three lines blink red like an exclamation mark at the fact no one has picked up the calls.

"At what point," Charlie says, "did I think it was a good idea to get multiple lines?"

At this, I laugh.

Mom gestures at the handset still sitting in the cradle. "Is Haley not here? Someone should get that. They might be tipsters."

Or lunatics.

"Gee, Mom," Charlie says, "perhaps we should have discussed that very thing before you released our number to the media. And, no, Haley isn't. Car trouble. The calls will go to voicemail. And, if we lose our assistant over this, I *will* kill you. This stunt just earned her a bigger Christmas bonus. And you're paying it."

Yikes. I can't remember the last time I saw Charlie this steamed at our mother.

The two lock eyes in a brutal stare-down. I have to give my sister credit for holding her temper. Anyone else would have skid marks by now.

"Alrighty." I smack my palms together. "What have we got here?"

I wedge myself between them and grab the top box off the pile. This might be just what I need today. A distraction.

From Galishea.

From Darcy.

From dead girls who deserved better than whatever hell they suffered before being dumped on the side of a road, where animals undoubtedly feasted on their dying flesh.

My God.

I set it on the table while the phone continues its assault on my tattered nerves.

It's going to be a long morning.

The blaring quiets—thank you—and immediately starts again, and everything inside my brain short-circuits.

I move to the credenza, run my fingers along the back of the phone, and yank the plug. The ringing still echoes from the reception area, but not nearly as loudly.

"Thank you," Mom says. "How annoying."

"Ha!" Charlie says with pure disbelief.

And then hers starts ringing. She holds it up so we can see the display.

JJ Carrington's flashing smile lights up the screen under the contact name "The Emperor."

"Excellent!" Charlie huffs. "He can't be happy."

She lowers the phone and stares at it for a split second. "Might as well get it over with." She stabs at it and lifts it to her ear. "Before you say anything, I'm sorry. My mother just got here. Let me call you back."

JJ's voice booms through the line, and Charlie flinches.

"Well," Mom says, her full throttle indignance smothering us. "If law enforcement had done something sooner, we wouldn't be in this situation."

JJ's yelling intensifies. Suddenly, my terror over Jerome hinting at marriage last night doesn't seem like such a huge event.

"JJ," Charlie says, her voice level. "I understand. Believe me, I'm not pleased with her either. But, I have to call you back."

More screaming, and Charlie gazes at the ceiling, draws a long breath, and does the only thing she can. She hangs up on The Emperor.

"Mom, you're totally killing me," she says. "Do you have any idea how hard that man works? His list of cases reaches the sky."

Before our mother can launch into one of her lectures about subpar police work, I clear my throat and gesture to the boxes. "What is all this?"

"You'll love it," Mom says, flipping a lid off one.

As she busies herself unloading files, I glance back at Charlie and her murderous glare. "I've got this," I say. "Go deal with JJ."

"I appreciate it, however, the best way to do that is to pummel him with information. Which I don't have."

"Well," Mom drawls, "if we'd stop wasting time, I could show you."

"Ha!" Charlie barks again, and all I can think is my mother might wind up in a body bag tonight.

After my sister bludgeons her.

My head is pounding. Between ghosts of dead women and Jerome's marriage hint, I'm spent.

I mean *marriage*?

It's not that I don't love Jerome. I do. He may not be JJ with his flashing smile, slick suits, and big-time job, but Jerome is … well … everything. Understanding when I need it. Loving when I need it.

Tough when I need it.

Jerome accepts and shares me with the dead when most men wouldn't.

And now he wants to marry me?

I glance at my mother, obsessed, brilliant, and the one who passed her passion to me, and reality smacks at me. I think about all my late nights. My getting lost in my work reconstructing the dead so we can find them justice.

Like Mom, I'm obsessed. Our methods might be different—Mom and her reporting versus me and my sculpting—but I have turned into her.

Dear God, please help me.

Jerome must be out of his mind. Why would anyone subject themselves to this chaos?

I shake it off. Chalk it up to sheer exhaustion. I need sleep. A lot of it. If I could squeeze even one ounce of reason from my strung-out mind, I'd march right out the door and go home.

Mom points at the boxes. "I have everything in here."

I keep my focus on her. I have to. If I look down, I'll get sucked in.

Sleep.

I need sleep.

The damned bleeping from reception continues. Dang, that phone is going wild.

Mom is in motion, hefting another box from her cart. "Meg, don't just stand there. Grab one. Let's get these on the table, and I'll show you what I have."

"No," Charlie says, her voice firm. "We have work to do. For our paying clients. This will have to wait."

Mom whirls. "A murdered eight-year-old and you're turning your back?"

Oh, boy. Wrong thing to say. I know my sister. If I don't intervene, this will turn into a...thing.

Familial unrest.

Which isn't exactly an odd occurrence. For years, my family has operated in a certain way. A certain way that involves Mom and me, the obsessed ones, bonding over cold cases, while Charlie and Dad, the remarkably level-headed and dare I say rational ones, try to talk us down.

The only way to keep this situation under control is to A) allow my mother to show me what is obviously extensive research, and B) get my sister out of here.

I face Charlie, whose expression is solid granite.

Oh. Boy.

"I've got this," I say. "I was about to take a break anyway. I'll organize it all and walk you through it later."

"Excellent plan!" Mom beams.

Charlie does her best to ignore our mother. "Meg, you should rest. You've been here all night."

I'm not about to admit that. No sense giving her ammunition.

And then I do the one thing I know I shouldn't.

I look at the two remaining boxes on the cart. This will be the distraction I need. The perfect excuse to avoid Jerome and his hypothetical suggestion of marriage.

A case, I'll tell him. Provided by our mother. The nut. It's almost too perfect. A new task for me to dive into, and hello, he knows when my mother is on a mission there's no denying her.

Talk about a double-whammy.

I remove the lid from the box. "I'm fine. The distraction will be good." I wave her off. "Just, you know, keep the coffee coming."

Charlie gives me ten long seconds of eye contact while Mom grabs the last box from the cart.

"We're good," I say. "Really, I'm fine."

She shakes her head and points. "Two hours. Then you need sleep."

Good luck, girlfriend. "Sure. No problem. And, please, deal with that phone. I can't take it."

"I'll turn the ringer down and ask Haley to go through the messages. We'll come up with a plan on how to manage it. Mom, if we lose Haley, you're helping me beg her to stay."

"Yada, yada," our mother says. "Whatever."

Clearly unhappy with us, my sister spins on her pricey heel and heads to the door.

"Maddening," she mutters. "The both of you."

Once Charlie clears out, I turn back to the box, staring down at the contents that nearly spill over the top. "Wow. Mom, what is all of this?"

She edges the box sideways. "That's box one. I labeled them."

Of course, she did.

"Witness statements. The Hartmans were having their annual Christmas bash. Two hundred of their closest friends."

"Two hundred!"

The Hartmans are one of those uber-wealthy D.C. families who aren't politicians but have enough money to ensure their candidate of choice is elected. Which bodes well for them, since their wealth is built on oil and gas, and they need politicians in their pocket.

"I haven't been able to put together the complete guest list," Mom says, "but I'm eighty percent there."

I lift a manila folder and open it. Inside is a half inch-thick, heavily redacted transcript of an interview with Irene Hartman, the now-deceased matriarch of the family and great-grandmother of the victim.

Some may think my mother is crazy, but she gets shit done. "Mom, how did you get this?"

"I FOIA'd it."

FOIA. The much-loved Freedom of Information Act allows citizens, particularly journalists, to request copies of records. And the government is required to release them. Sure, there are certain exceptions, but for the most part, unless a government entity wants to battle a lawsuit, they have to comply.

My mother loves a good FOIA request.

"Go, Mom."

Anxious to see what she's collected, I set the folder on the conference room table and flip through articles and news clippings. A photo of a smiling Tiffany, her two front teeth missing. It's like a knife to my chest. I set the image aside and ... whoa.

"The nine-one-one call," I say.

"Yes. That's one of the few that wasn't redacted. The bastards. Mary Hartman made it. She took over when Irene died."

That name. I spin it around, thinking, thinking, thinking.

Folder in hand, I step to the doorway. "Charlie!"

"What?" my sister calls from her office.

"Mary Hartman. How do I know that name?"

"One of JJ's deputies is a Hartman. Mary is his mother. Her brother-in-law, Ron Hartman, runs Hartman Oil and Gas."

Yes!

I hustle to Charlie's office and find her behind her desk, pounding away on her laptop. "What's the deputy's first name?"

Still typing, she peers up at me. "Alex. JJ likes him. Hard worker. He's helped out on a few of the cold cases."

"Mom has a transcript of the nine-one-one call Mary made that night."

Finally, Charlie stops typing, a sly smile easing across her face. "She FOIA'd it. God bless her. If I weren't so mad, I'd applaud."

"She's got interviews, press clippings, the whole works. Do you think Alex Hartman might talk to us?"

"Well, with a family member being the victim, one would hope."

"Can you grease the wheels with JJ?"

"That would require talking to him. The Schocks aren't high on his list right now."

Ouch.

I scrunch my nose. "Sorry."

"It's certainly not your fault."

I lean against the doorframe. "What if I call him?"

"JJ?"

"He can scream at me all he wants. I don't have to live with him, so to speak."

Charlie narrows her eyes, clearly considering this strategy. "He won't yell at you. He adores you."

I copy my sister's sly smile from a minute ago. "Exactly."

She slides her desk phone in my direction. "Have at it. Let's see just how mad The Emperor really is."

3

Charlie

Cold case clearance rates have been dropping for four decades. Unsolved murders are at an all-time high.

JJ doesn't answer his direct line. After multiple rings, it directs me to his voicemail.

Meg leaves a brief message. "Hi, JJ. It's your favorite forensic artist. Call me back when you have a chance?"

He won't.

From outside comes the scraping of the snow shovel Matt is wielding in his crusade against the storm. The sound makes my teeth itch. He's been at it for half an hour. Or maybe I'm just out of patience with everything.

Haley is drowning in calls. She's fielded a dozen quacks who claim they know the killer, a man demanding a million dollars or he'll start picking off the Hartmans, and two psychics who swear Tiffany's ghost named names. All they want in return is a little national spotlight. Each insists that she has revealed the identity and whereabouts of the killer—all Mom needs to do is get them an interview with a major news outlet, and they'll tell all.

The cherry on top is the woman who believes she *is* Tiffany. Reincarnated, I guess, since she's only nineteen. She's asked to join our mother's crusade. She plans to chain herself to the Hartmans' gate until the Feds give her justice. For her own murder? Yep, it boggles the mind.

After forwarding all the messages containing threats or potential leads—no matter how small—to the local PD and CCing my former coworkers at the FBI, where I worked long hours for very little pay, profiling, but loved every minute of it, I contact my favorite hacker, Teeg. I put in a request for him to take down that damn social media video and temporarily block my mother from her account. It only costs me tickets to the next Comic Con. A small price to pay.

"Call JJ's cell," Meg orders.

I snort. "He'll know it's me. He won't answer." I dial the main office line, and we get JJ's assistant, Carolyn. Meg requests to speak to him. "He's in a meeting," Carolyn informs her. "I'll let him know you called."

Even my sister is getting the brush off.

Since we're on speaker, I can't resist butting in. "You're deflecting, Carolyn. It's essential we speak to him. We'll hold until he's done."

She's the model of professionalism, which is why I can hear the sigh she doesn't let out. "I'm afraid you'll be holding a long time, then. You're the reason he's in the meeting. I'll inform him you called, and I'm sure he'll contact you at his earliest convenience."

Right. "What do you mean he's in the meeting because of me?"

"Not you, per se, Charlize," she corrects, using my full name in that annoying way that JJ does when goading me. "The

Schock women have stirred up a hornet's nest with Mary Hartman, and now JJ has to deal with her, her lawyer, and her fixer. Have a nice day."

She disconnects.

Meg arches a brow. I shrug. "He may adore you, but he's pissed at all of us. Even more so if he's in that meeting."

"You did hang up on him earlier."

"He earned it."

Screech. Fingers on a chalkboard. I suspect Matt's done, but staying outside gives him an excuse to avoid us. I don't blame him. "If Mary Hartman has brought in her lawyer and a fixer..." My stomach falls. "Fallyn."

Meg makes a face.

Fallyn Pasche. The top 'fixer' in D.C. handles scandals for the rich and powerful, and she's sleeping with one of the Justice Team.

A lawyer and a fixer. All of my red flags run up the pole and salute. What does Mary have to hide?

"God. Fallyn will slap a restraining order on Mom before we can say Merry Christmas," Meg says.

Mom stomps in. "Doesn't matter. JJ and the Hartmans better get used to seeing my face because this is just the beginning." She tugs on her coat. "I'm going to his office. Coming?"

I shoot to my feet. "You are not."

"Mary Hartman is there. I want to speak to her. She's refused my offers to sit down and discuss what happened and won't return my calls. I'll ambush her at JJ's."

Even Meg knows this is a bad idea. She puts a hand on Mom's arm. "We still have boxes to sort through."

Mom snugs a knitted cap on her head. "You stay here and work on that."

Haley swings into the doorway and pulls up short. She's wearing a sweater dress and knee-high boots. Her hair is in a low ponytail. Since last summer, I've given her more responsibilities around here. She's good at details and is highly logical. Plus, with her blond hair and blue eyes, she's effective at getting guys to talk. We've closed several cheating spouse cases in record time since I trained her how to use her psych degree and those pretty eyes to gain confessions.

She lowers her voice. "There's a reporter in the waiting room who wants to talk to Helen."

Mom's eyes light up. "From which outlet?"

Haley checks the tablet in her hand. "The Washington Post, and a second reporter called from Channel 4—a Denise Brown —requesting a quote on what Schock Investigations is doing about the case."

Mom is instantly out of her coat and whipping off her hat. She pats her silver hair into place. "The Post? Don't just stand there, girl. Show our visitor to the conference room. He'll need coffee."

Haley blinks. "Did you just call me 'girl?'"

Wincing, Meg deftly steers Mom out of my office while I walk Haley back to her desk. "I'm so, so sorry. Ignore her."

The reporter paces our small waiting room in a navy sweater over a white dress shirt and tie, pocketing his cell phone when he spots me. "Dr. Schock, isn't it?" He extends a hand. His graying hair is slicked back, and he still has a scarf draped around his neck, even though he's discarded his coat into one of the two chairs. "Robert Beechum. Call me Bob. I was hoping to speak to you about—"

"Yes, I know." I debate shooing him off, but maybe I can use this opportunity to our advantage. I accept his handshake. His fingers are cold, his skin dry. "Did you investigate Tiffany's murder when it happened?"

He narrows keen eyes at me. "Before my time, I'm afraid."

"Who worked the homicide desk back then?"

"Lots of people."

A non-answer. The investigative reporter prefers to be the

one asking the questions. Should I offer him a deal if he works with us? I don't have enough facts yet to put myself in that hole. "How about a cup of coffee?"

He knows the offer is more than a formality. He stays on my good side and we do discover something? He'll gather key facts for his story and enhance his credibility within the news community. "I'd like that. Is your mother here?"

The thought of turning her loose with him makes me pause. It's my best option at the moment, though, to keep her from going to JJ's office—inevitable Armageddon if that happens. "You do realize she's a reporter, too. She writes for the Crime Desk at the D.C. Investigative Journal." Not high-profile, and her articles rarely receive more than a few comments now and then, but she takes her job very seriously. "She'll purposely mislead you because she plans to be the one to break open this case."

He's undaunted. "My angle is more about the resurgence of cold case groups. What motivates them. What drives them." The words flow off his tongue as if he's practiced this speech. Cue the pitch. "Across the country this year, several have been instrumental in assisting overworked and underfunded police departments solve important investigations."

Yep, there it is. While all of that may be accurate, I'm skeptical that's his motivation. If he can get the scoop on who murdered Tiffany, it will make his career.

He must realize, however, that what I said is true—Mom likes publicity, but she wants to be the one who solves this whale of a cold case. She won't share that trophy with him or any of his colleagues. "Titillating story there," I mutter.

He frowns.

Matt comes in from outside, looking like a model for a ski resort as he shakes snow from his hair. He rakes his fingers through the thick strands, and it stands straight up, but appears as though he styled it that way on purpose.

I hate him and his shampoo commercial hair. Mine is always a disaster—if I get a blowout, it instantly frizzes. If I try to put curls in it, they fall flat. Most of the time, I just keep it in a ponytail and forget about it.

"The snow is easing," Matt says. "Are we still having our morning meeting?"

"Pushing it to tomorrow." I have to leave shortly to get across town for that trial, and Meg needs a nap. If she doesn't crash soon, she's going to start hallucinating.

Moot point. It'll never happen. *Better to keep her busy.*

Matt introduces himself to Bob, and they exchange a couple comments about the weather. The phone calls have slowed, and Haley hands me a stack of blue message slips. "My ear's filing a hostile work complaint."

"Noted." I don't look at the slips as I lead Bob to the conference room. Meg is gathering all of the papers and shoving them into their boxes. Mom already has two steaming mugs of coffee waiting and gives Bob a huge smile.

More introductions, and I help Meg finish removing the case information from sight before I drag her across the hall to my office. "I have to testify in the Costnick trial at the Moultrie Courthouse."

"I'm not going anywhere. I'll run interference with Mom."

"That courthouse takes me right past the U.S. Attorney's building."

She gives me a curious look. "And?"

"If the man we want to talk to won't come to the phone..."

She grins, getting my meaning. "We show up in person."

"Maybe we can chat with Alex, too. Get some perspective on what he remembers about that night."

"I like this plan."

It's a terrible plan, but I like it, too.

Matt appears in the doorway. "Can I come?"

"Don't you have the Anderson case to review?" I ask.

"Closed it last night. I couldn't sleep, and a deep dive into a hunch paid off."

"Good for you," Meg says. "I couldn't sleep either."

He squeezes her shoulder. "We'll both do better tonight."

She gives him a wan smile. Wishful thinking.

"You drive," I tell Matt, tossing him my keys. "Meg and I need to come up with a strategy for JJ. And another for Alex."

"What if we run into Mary?" Meg asks. "Or Fallyn?"

Matt pauses. "What's Fallyn got to do with this?"

"Maybe nothing." I relay what Carolyn told us and our assumption about Fallyn being on the Hartman payroll. "That's why I want our ducks in a row. We may only get one shot at Mary, and we better make it count. If we do encounter her, follow my lead, okay?"

"What are you going to do?" Matt asks.

I flash him a grin. "How many red-blooded women can resist you and your muscles, Mad Dog? You handle Mary. Meg and I will handle Alex."

He gives a fake shudder. "I feel so objectified."

Meg laughs, and the sound makes me smile for real.

Haley is horrified that we're abandoning her. The calls have stopped, though. *Thank you, Teeg.* I tell her to take the rest of the day off, an early Christmas present. She's relieved. We sneak out, leaving Mom and Bob to themselves.

I hope it's not a colossal mistake—a King Kong versus Godzilla-level mistake.

Traffic moves at a snail's pace, snowplows and pileups making things worse. The only positive is that Meg, Matt, and I come up with a dozen questions and theories to investigate further.

By the time we arrive at Carolyn's desk, Mom has figured out we've abandoned her. My phone is filled with accusatory texts and voicemails.

Wait until she realizes what I had done to her TikTok account.

"I told you, he's in a meeting," Carolyn snips, looking at our trio over the top of her reading glasses. "He doesn't have time to speak to you."

"We're not here for him," I say. We've cooked up a story that we need Fallyn's services. Not a stretch if Mom continues to escalate. And since she's not answering our texts, we need to make sure she hasn't handcuffed herself to someone's radiator. "We're here to see—"

"Charlie?" All three of us turn. Alex Hartman strides across the blue carpet toward us.

He and JJ have contests to see who's the best dressed. The office staff votes. Could go either way today—Alex is rocking his charcoal suit and classy forest green tie.

He hands a file to Carolyn and mutters, "The Galishea Tern wrap-up." She nods, tucking the file into a stack of others. He pats my elbow. "Here to see JJ?"

"No." While Mom likes to tackle things with lots of fanfare, I prefer a subtler approach. "First off, let me apologize for our mother's way of handling this." I sound more contrite than I feel, but sometimes that's what the situation calls for. I gesture at my companions. "This is my sister, Meg, by the way, and our lead investigator, Matt. We have an appointment at the courthouse and needed to stop here on the way. I'm glad we caught you. Meg and I had no idea our mother was going to stir all this up."

When Meg and I were young, we enjoyed watching old cartoons. Wonder Twins was a favorite. To enable their powers, the duo touched their fists together and said, "Wonder Twin powers, activate!" Throughout our lives, we've used the phrase as a sort of code when we were up to no good.

It's like she's reading my mind, and our voices mingle telepathically. She gives Alex an apologetic smile and lays a hand on his arm. She's the touchy-feely part of our Wonder duo, and she turns on the empathy. "I'm sure this is a sad time for your family. All this renewed publicity must be hard on you, especially with the holidays approaching. I can't imagine how distressing it must be, and here our mother is, right in the middle of it."

For a few heartbeats, he doesn't move, meeting each of our eyes with a cool appraisal. He exudes privilege and confidence, a man at the height of his professional career from a prestigious D.C. family. As if coming to a decision, he gestures for us to follow him across the hall. "Why don't we take this to my office?"

Gotcha. Hook, line, and…

Meg gives me a look behind his back. I hold out a fist. She taps it.

"Wonder Twin powers activate," I whisper. The first stage of our plan, *Interrogate Alex Hartman*, is underway.

4

Meg

We follow Alex to his office, filing in while Matt takes up the rear.

The space is a shoebox—barely wide enough to hold all of us—and exactly what I expected: bland gray walls, a metal-framed desk, and a crowded bookshelf in the corner. Most likely law books, given the setting.

Charlie takes one of the guest chairs, also metal, in front of the desk. I take the other, while Matt leans against the wall to my right.

After we're seated, Alex waves a hand at the door. "Would you mind closing that?"

"Sure," Matt says, stepping sideways to do as asked.

Alex, tall and lean, sits back in his chair. "I appreciate you coming by, and your apology. Obviously, this case creates stress for my family. My mother, particularly."

His mother? Tiffany's aunt? What about her parents?

Typical. The Hartmans are masters of self-promotion. So self-consumed.

I'm not denying their pain, but how about even an ounce of sympathy for Tiffany's immediate family?

Suddenly, all eyes are on me, and my sister gives me a WTF glare. I must have made a noise or some other signal of my irritation.

Charlie, being Charlie, swings back to Alex. "I can imagine the attention is unnerving. Believe me, I know how persistent our mother can be. This is why we've agreed to help her in her pursuits."

Alex's eyebrows hitch a tad higher. "Help her? As in investigate?"

"Yes," I say. "As you know, we specialize in this sort of thing, and the sooner we can get into it, maybe we can help find your cousin's killer."

"That," Alex says, "would be amazing. We've hired investigators over the years, but unfortunately, nothing has panned out."

"Perhaps now, with all the advancements in DNA testing and getting the word out via social media, something will pop."

"The online sleuths. Sometimes they make me insane."

"Half of them are quacks," Charlie says. "But some? Damned good. You never know."

He lifts a hand. "How can I help?"

Excellent. I lean forward. "Could you take us through what you remember from that night?"

"Of course. But, unfortunately, I don't know that it'll help. There were over two hundred people there. I was only nine and just wanted to get to the presents. I didn't like all the people in the house. It wasn't, still isn't, my thing."

"Do you remember where you were when Tiffany was found?"

He glances in Matt's direction. "You don't forget something

like that. I was upstairs in the study with two of my friends. Playing video games. I'd just gotten a new PlayStation." He smiles wistfully. "Life was simple then. After that night, everything changed."

"I'm sure," I say. "Tragedy blows up your world."

He meets my gaze. "You sound like you understand."

"Not in the intimate way you've experienced, but I've been through traumatic events. Plus, when I was in sixth grade, nine kids from our area went missing. They've never been found. Fear and paranoia gripped me. I still have nightmares."

"I'm sorry," he says, his voice soft and kind.

Feeling the punch of the memories, I shake my head. "Like you, it was a long time ago."

"What about," Charlie begins, "the investigation? From what we know, there were a lot of people involved."

"I've gone over the files and reports a dozen times," he says. "Frankly, it's a mess. Procedures back then weren't as rigid as they are now, and, let's face it, the local PD wasn't exactly experienced in homicides."

I know this, just from my surface knowledge of the case, is true. First responders, in an effort to offer aid to Tiffany, trampled through the crime scene, leaving mud, finger and footprints, and DNA all over the place.

I'd heard about this from Mom just this morning. Her outrage over the contamination. "Given your familiarity, what are your thoughts about the possibility of reopening the case?"

"It's still an open cold case. We simply haven't had any new evidence that would warrant putting an investigator on it full-time. All the evidence collected so far has been reviewed, including by me. If I thought something was missed, I'd be all over it. I can promise you that."

Beside me, Matt shifts, angling his body and propping a shoulder against the wall. "You mentioned the DNA. It's been thirty years. There's a genetic genealogy research lab we use.

They have cutting-edge technology. Why not bring them in? See what they can and can't do with what you have."

"We've discussed it," he says.

"And?"

He swings his gaze to me. "It's expensive." His hand immediately goes up. "From a government funding perspective. We can't ask taxpayers to take that on. And, yes, my family has money. We've discussed it, though my mother has concerns about giving my aunt and uncle false hope."

Oh. Puh-lease. False hope, my butt. Mary Hartman, matriarch of the famed Hartman clan, wants to avoid the very thing my mother has just done.

Media frenzy.

Reporters hanging out at the Hartman gate and annoying the snooty neighbors who want to keep the riffraff out.

"You have to agree," I say, "the lack of closure on this case is a stain on not only the police department but the DA's office as well. Not to mention getting justice for your cousin."

My sister reaches for me, giving my arm a gentle squeeze. She wants me to back off. To tone it down.

Catch more flies with honey.

I've always hated that saying.

Still, she might be right here. Alienating a Deputy DA, not to mention a family member of the victim, might not be my best approach.

I shake off my thoughts. "Sorry," I blurt. "I'm tired, and these unsolved cases, particularly ones involving children, get me riled."

Alex's dark eyes meet my gaze. "No apology necessary. I completely understand. Doing what I do, it's hard to stomach."

"What about the panic room?" Matt asks. "What was the deal with that?"

Alex shifts to Matt. "It was a safety measure. My mother's idea, in case we had an emergency. There's an underground tunnel that connects to a cottage on the property. Say, in case of a fire or an intruder, we had an escape."

How very Clue-like.

Charlie makes a slow circle with her hand. "So, it could be used as a safe room or an escape route?"

"Right. Though we've never had to use it."

An underground tunnel? Was that really necessary? I mean, these people were rich, but it wasn't as if the president was in residence.

"Forgive me," I say, "but it seems kind of ..."

"Extreme?" Alex adds helpfully with a faint chuckle. "It is. It was. At the time, my family was receiving threats due to Hartman Enterprises' financial issues and necessary layoffs. As Charlie knows, there are many unstable individuals out there. Our security team proposed the safe room idea, and my mother implemented it."

"But the project was still under construction then?"

"It was. After the murder, my mother was more determined than ever. At the time of Tiff's death, it had been dug out but not finished."

"So," Charlie says, "someone could have walked through it and reached the house?"

"As I recall, the actual opening connecting the tunnel to the panic room hadn't been completed. They wouldn't have been able to access the house that way."

Alex pauses, clears his throat, and for just a second, he presses his lips together. It's barely visible, but his prosecutorial mask, that refined demeanor, finally slips. The conversation, all this talk about his dead cousin, is catching up with him. Crumbling his emotional walls.

Like me, he was a child forced to deal with tragedy, and that never leaves you.

Charlie sits forward, resting her hand on the edge of the desk. "I'm sorry to have to ask you these questions."

"It's fine. A new set of eyes might do us some good. Even the smallest details sometimes make a difference."

A buzzing sound interrupts us. Charlie reaches into her coat pocket, sliding her phone free. She holds it up so I can view the screen, and I once again see JJ's handsome face.

I jerk my head to the door, and she rises from her seat. "Excuse me. It's JJ."

She hustles out.

"So," Matt says. "Tiffany. What can you tell us about her?"

Alex smiles. "She was just a normal kid. She had these crazy blonde curls we used to tease her about. She wanted to be a hairstylist when she grew up." He lets out a soft chuckle. "When she'd sleep over, my mother would let her brush her hair at night. I can still picture her standing behind the sofa with that boar bristle brush in her hand."

"My apologies for having to ask this, but...could the attack have been sexual in nature? Was that ever looked into?"

Alex nods. "Every man at that party was investigated. Unfortunately, security cameras hadn't been installed inside yet. Only the exterior. It was on the list of things to do while the panic room was under construction."

"So, there's no footage of her going into the basement?"

He shakes his head. "No. And why would she? The party and presents were upstairs. There's nothing of her leaving the house, either. There are hours of tape, but they can't find anything on her."

"That's odd," I say.

"As I said, there were two hundred there, and she was a child. She could have gotten lost in the crowd."

"Maybe," Matt muses. "Could we get copies of the footage? I'd like to take a look. With the advancements in facial recognition, I have a friend who might be able to help us."

His friend, I'm sure, would be Teeg from the Justice Team. We often joke that computers are no match for Teeg.

"I'll talk to JJ. If he signs off on it, I'll get it to you. Any assistance you could provide would be greatly appreciated. From a business and personal standpoint. Obviously, I'd like to get this case solved. I don't know if you'll find anything. We've been over the files hundreds of times."

I push to my feet. "Well, like you said. A fresh set of eyes never hurt."

5

———————

Charlie

My heart races as I step out of Alex's office, my phone buzzing insistently in my hand. I try to infuse calm into my simple greeting, "Hey, JJ. Thanks for getting back to me."

"Charlize, we need to talk. Now."

Power exudes from those six words. When *I* want to talk, he ghosts me. When *he* wants to? It's an order.

My hackles go up.

Mom, you owe me.

I lower my voice and run through my options: flirt, tease, logic. I pick the latter. "I know you're upset, and yes, Mom overstepped, but we're all in it now, so can we make the best of it?"

"The brass is breathing down my neck." Yep, that's a 'no.' "They want this ridiculous publicity to go away." His words land like a hammer, pounding his frustration into me. "My bosses, the Hartmans, the chief of police. The mayor, Charlie.

Mary Hartman is a friend of his. And, worse, he has to see her at some charity gig tonight. Great timing, there. No one is happy about Helen and her goofball group making this a public spectacle again."

Yes, I've called them goofballs myself—but they mean well, and someone has to defend them. Accusing him of name-calling won't help my mission.

If JJ's flailing this hard, the pressure must be nuclear. And if they're this desperate to shut us down... what exactly are they hiding? "JJ, we can't just—"

The hammer is replaced with a steel-edged knife. "I'm walking a tightrope here. One wrong move—even speaking to you in private like this about the case—and it could cost me my job."

Is he serious? "Who said that?"

"Doesn't matter. If that happens, I can guarantee that Tiffany and her family will never get closure. The killer will never be caught. No matter what your mother pulls, she'll only end up in a jail cell."

That thought leaves me speechless. We've investigated cold cases before, but none that unleashed this much upheaval or these kinds of threats. What is going on here? Yes, the public outcry is leading the charge at the moment, but if I didn't know better, I'd think JJ's office and possibly the Hartmans have something to hide.

Do they?

I close my eyes and picture him in his designer suit, pacing. His tall frame is no doubt taut with tension, and those blue-gray eyes I love are stormy with conflicting emotions. He may love playing the political games his position requires, but he loves justice more. He takes his role as the Emperor of Cold Cases as seriously as my mother does hers as an investigative journalist.

I don't need logic when I reply this time. "What do you

need from me? I'm trying to contain Mom, but you know how she is."

"Just...be careful. Watch your step. The killer is still out there. All this publicity could bring them out of the shadows. And if he believes any of us are getting close to uncovering his identity, he could come after us."

The warning in his tone is clear. Internally, I hear Matt's screeching shovel on the sidewalk again. "Understood. We'll tread lightly." But the warning in his tone lingers. He's right. We'll have to be smart and make sure Mom doesn't end up with a target on her back. At least, not a bigger one than she's already put there.

But I'm not about to let this case go, no matter what obstacles JJ's superiors throw in our path. And if the Hartmans want to bury the truth, they're going to have to bury me with it. "Just so you and I are clear—Schock Investigations is investigating Tiffany's unsolved murder. You know as well as I do that Mom and Meg have dug in their heels. I'm in it, whether you like it or not."

Dead silence.

My phone buzzes with a second call. District of Columbia Court System. Dammit—I'm almost out of time to get to the courthouse. "Can you hold for a quick sec?"

He hangs up.

Okay, then.

I answer and an automated voice tells me the trial has been postponed. No explanation is given. Judges don't take snow days. Something's off.

A follow-up text from the attorney who hired me states that the judge was involved in an accident and is currently at the hospital. An alternate hasn't been found. More details to come. My suspicious mind immediately wonders, was it an accident?

God, I'm paranoid.

Alex's door opens. Meg and Matt approach.

"Charlie?" Meg's voice is soft. "What's wrong?"

Alex accompanies them. "Bet I know," he says with a wink.

My retort dies on my lips as JJ rounds the corner. He zeroes in on us like a bullet. No hiding the fact now. With a tense sigh, he jerks his head toward his office, a clear command to follow.

"Good luck," Alex whispers.

Oh, joy. This should be fun. I silently fall into step behind JJ but can't keep up with his long legs. Like obedient soldiers, Meg and Matt follow, equally as silent.

His office is a stark contrast to Alex's. Plush carpet, cool colors, bold artwork on the walls. Just like JJ: dramatic but calculated. We both hesitate to sit—a subtle power play. I plant my feet, spine straight, as I meet my boyfriend's steely gaze. The eyes I love, usually dancing with mischief, hold a vicious storm.

He looms over his mahogany desk. "This ends now."

If only I could order Mom around like that. "If we don't find closure for that family, it will never be over."

"She's right," Meg insists. "Mom is onto something. I can feel it in my bones."

JJ's stern gaze shifts to her. "Your bones don't dictate policy, Meg."

My sister flinches and locks her jaw.

"Maybe they should," I shoot back, annoyance getting the better of me. "Right now, your policies are standing between us and justice."

JJ's jaw clenches, a muscle ticking beneath his skin. I see the gears turning in that brilliant mind of his, weighing options, calculating risks. He rattles off the same excuses to Meg and Matt that he gave me over the phone—his bosses, the Hartmans, the fact that his office has reviewed the case many times and found nothing new. Blah, blah, blah. The theory that the killer may target Mom gets their attention, as it did me. He knows how to hit the right triggers to give us all pause.

Meg goes to his expansive window with its view of the city.

The corners are frosty, much like the atmosphere of the room. "We're sorry for the trouble, JJ. Truly. But you have to understand why this matters so much to me—" She corrects herself. "Us."

I bite back a frustrated sigh. Now isn't the time for apologies. We need to push forward, not backpedal.

I hold my tongue.

Meg continues. Her empathy worked on Alex. It might on JJ. "We know you're in a difficult position. But please, can't we find a way to work together on this?"

I watch JJ's face for any crack in his resolve, and yep, I catch a glimpse of the man behind the title—torn, conflicted, but ultimately bound by restrictive rules—both official and the unspoken ones that are every bit as powerful in this building.

I hold my breath.

JJ's shoulders lower almost imperceptibly. He runs a hand through his dark hair, mussing it, but unlike Matt's, his falls back into perfect layers. "Damn it," he mutters. "It's dangerous. This isn't just about reopening a case. It's about admitting we're incompetent. The system failed, and the killer is still free. A killer who's again in the limelight and might strike out to protect him or herself. And you all are in the middle of this shit show."

"Sometimes, admitting we're wrong is the bravest thing we can do" I say, "and the Schocks don't back down from killers."

JJ's laugh is sharp, humorless. He paces behind his desk, unbuttoning his suit jacket to reveal the crisp, navy blue shirt underneath. "Christ, Charlie. I'm trying to protect you—professionally and personally. Helen's stunt has half of D.C. breathing down our necks. If I give the okay, there's no backtracking..."

"If you don't get on board—and we're right—it'll blow up bigger."

He hates it when I'm right, especially when being so means he's not. He braces his hands on the polished wood of his desk, and I see the burden of his position, of those expectations. His need to protect me and Meg—not to mention our mother—weighs down his broad shoulders.

Even amid this argument, I want to run my fingers over them.

As if it pains him, he relents. A little. "I'll do what I can to support your investigation, but I'll need your full cooperation. You follow my rules and the department's policies." He gives my sister a pointed look. "Regardless of your bones."

She smiles.

I fight a grin.

He straightens. "We frame it as a review. I'll tell the higher-ups it's damage control, a way to placate the public without admitting fault. No family interviews unless there's a damn good reason."

JJ in his element—navigating the treacherous waters of bureaucracy.

"No grand announcements, no promises we can't keep," he continues. "We review the evidence quietly, and if—*if*—we find something substantial, we reassess."

Meg nods, relieved. "Thank you, JJ."

We have our feet in the door. Now, we have to find a way to blow that door wide open.

Without Mom ending up in jail.

Or worse.

Matt scratches his stubble. "Speaking of evidence..."

JJ's eyes narrow. "What about it?"

"There's the matter of the security footage. From the night of the murder," I add. "Mom doesn't have it, and we need to view it."

His shoulders tighten, a flicker of frustration crossing his features. "I've never seen it." He catches the surprise on my face. "My deputies watched it," he says as if to cover for the lapse. "I'll ask Alex to dig it up and make a copy. We'll review it again together. But don't expect to find anything groundbreaking. Cold cases are cold for a reason."

He truly believes we're on a wild goose chase. Part of me wonders if he's right.

"Good. Working together is always better than being at each other's throats."

JJ sits, and even that exudes power. "Tonight? Say seven? My day is packed until then."

"Sounds good." Meg nods, happy at his offer. "Let's meet at Charlie's."

"Without Helen," JJ insists.

Tall order.

"I'll figure out a way to keep her away." I steel myself for the next uphill battle. "There's one more thing. We need clearance for new DNA testing."

His eyes snap. His voice stays low, controlled. "Do you have any idea what kind of red tape that involves? The expense?"

"Schock Investigations will use our lab and pay for it." No clue where I'll find the money. Maybe Mom can start a GoFundMe. "With the latest advances in genome matching, it could break the case wide open. We can't ignore—"

"I'm aware of what we can and can't ignore." He looks like he's mentally planning my funeral. "As I stated, we start with the records and security video. That's all."

"For now," Meg says.

He glares at her. She just keeps smiling.

Death wish, that one.

The DNA testing is crucial. If JJ won't give us official clearance...

A plan forms in my mind, a risky and potentially career-ending one. Meg will love it.

"Understood." I'm not lying. I do understand, but I'm not agreeing to back down. "We'll focus on the other stuff."

The unsaid 'for now' hangs in the air.

JJ narrows his eyes, suspicious of my sudden acquiescence. His phone rings, and Carolyn tells him he's needed in a meeting. He acknowledges he'll be there momentarily, then hustles us out.

He escorts us into the elevator and all the way to the ground floor. It's as if he doesn't trust us to leave. "We'll reconvene tonight," he says, holding the doors open so he can return upstairs. His tone is less commanding now. "I'll bring pizza."

For a moment, I see a flicker of the man I love—the one who laughs at my terrible jokes and challenges me to ridiculous bets.

"Thank you," Meg says. "We won't let you—or Tiffany—down."

No smile, no nod, and I'm left hollow. Meg must sense my unease and squeezes my arm.

A commotion reaches us as we cross the expansive lobby.

Matt frowns. "What's that noise?"

Extra security guards swarm in from other parts of the building. Outside the entrance doors, it's chaos.

"Oh my God," Meg gasps.

A sea of people floods the snowy lawns and sidewalks. They're spilling into the street, causing drivers to honk and yell. Signs wave in the air, demanding justice, and they chant various ill-rhyming slogans.

At the center of it all stands a familiar figure—Helen Schock.

My stomach twists. "For the love of all that's holy."

News vans roll up, reporters and cameras spilling out. As we watch, Mom raises a bullhorn, her voice blasting over the noise. "Tiffany deserves justice!" The crowd goes wild. She has to wait a few seconds before she can be heard again. "We won't be silenced until she has it!"

I pull out my phone and dial.

"Who are you calling?" Meg asks.

"A lawyer," I say. "She's going to need it."

Matt eyes a patrol car, easing its way toward the throng. "It's a peaceful protest. I doubt they'll arrest—"

A large man with a handmade sign lunges off the sidewalk and smacks the patrol car with it. The lights come on, and the siren blips.

I meet Matt's chagrined glance. "You were saying?"

"Hell no, we won't go!" Mom yells. Her mob picks up the chant. She leads the pack toward the entrance. The two police officers and the security guards suddenly have more on their hands than they can control.

"Will they really put her in jail?" Meg asks.

For her own safety, I almost hope they do. Iris, the attorney's receptionist, answers on the second ring. "Charlie Schock," I tell her. "Put me through to Daniel Messing. Now."

"Good morning, Ms. Schock. What is this regarding?"

I watch an officer try to take the bullhorn from Mom. She resists. Two of her supporters attempt to help her, and the whole lot tumbles to the sidewalk a few feet from us.

"My mother," I tell Iris. "She's about to be arrested."

6

Meg

"Really?" I ask, staring at my mother across the table in a small interview room at the jail. Matt says they don't call them interrogation rooms. It's apparently not a good look, so they opt for the more politically correct phrasing.

Mom, haughty indignance on full display, lifts her chin. "What was I supposed to do? Sit around and wait for justice?"

"Mom! Dad is beside himself. He got halfway here, and we told him to go home. The only reason they even let us see you is because JJ pulled strings. You owe him a thank you for that."

At this, Mom scowls at me, then shifts her gaze to Charlie, sitting beside me. "He's a good man. I'm sorry to aggravate him."

"I feel a *but* coming," Charlie says.

Mom nods. "He's dragged his heels on this."

Like a rogue wave building in front of me, a massive energy

rises as Mom and Charlie glare at each other. The tension is thick enough to lock my shoulders up.

"Mom?" I say. "That's not fair, and you know it. Keep this up, and we may leave you here."

"You wouldn't dare."

"Try me," Charlie says. "And, oh, by the way, the lawyer I got you is on his way. But you might as well get comfortable in that cell because it's probably too late to get you an arraignment today. Plan on spending the night."

That thought literally sickens me. Our mother will be forced to stay with God knows what kind of lowlifes. Then again, she'll probably befriend a hooker and crackhead.

If Mom is dejected by this information, she doesn't show it.

In her mind, it's good for her cause. A way to rile the public over the establishment forcing a retiree to sleep in a cell.

JJ called it. This is a full-blown shit show.

"What have you girls done on the case?"

Her tone is almost accusatory. As if we've nothing better to do than champion her cause.

At this, Charlie snorts. "Oh, not much." She rolls her hand. "Other than getting JJ to agree to a quiet look at the case. We're reviewing the evidence tonight."

"Finally," Mom huffs. "What about DNA testing?"

"Not yet," I say. "We'll get there."

Mom rolls her eyes. "All right. Well, if I were you, I'd start with Mary Hartman. Go to the queen herself."

"No."

Charlie's tone is so matter of fact, Mom's head snaps back. "Pardon?"

"The family is off-limits."

"Damn JJ." Mom mutters. "Still pulling the strings."

I grin at my mother. "He is the U.S. Attorney, Mom."

She blows air through her lips. "I'll figure something out

there. But, I have to say, that's ridiculous. How does he expect us to solve it if we can't talk to them?"

Charlie pins our mother with a look. "You've created a political firestorm. And that was before you got arrested. The mayor himself stopped by to speak with JJ this morning. He has to see Helen at a fundraiser tonight and was none too happy."

Curious, I cock my head. "What fundraiser?"

"I have no idea," Charlie says.

Mom waves a hand. "It's probably to support families in need during the holidays. Mary is all about Christmas. This might be our shot at her. She'll be distracted and surrounded by people. If ever there was a chance to catch her off guard, this is it. Meg, call Audrey at The Ledger. She has a contact in the mayor's office. She knows who you are. Tell her I need to know where the mayor is going tonight."

Go, Mom. "Wow," I say. "That's impressive."

"You may think I'm a zealot, pushing my ideas on you, but I get things done."

"No," Charlie states in that same definitive tone from a few minutes ago. "I'm not going."

I swing to Charlie. "I could go. Maybe take Matt with me. We find Mary and..."

"Are you insane? JJ will kill me. Kill us! We've just gotten him to agree to this review, and now, on day one, you want to risk it?"

I sure do.

"We can say we bought the tickets before all this happened."

"He'll never believe that."

"We can claim we purchased them yesterday, thinking it might be an opportunity to speak to the family. Since we had the tickets, we felt we might as well go. Even though we don't—wink, wink—intend on speaking to the family."

"And what about convening tonight? What am I supposed to tell him?"

"Charlize," Mom says, "do what you do. The man is putty in your hands."

Wait. What? Is our mother telling Charlie, her oldest daughter, to manipulate JJ with sex?

A gagging noise erupts from my throat. "Ew."

"Oh, please." Mom rolls her eyes. "Men are idiots when it comes to sex."

"I really am not believing this," Charlie says.

She rises from the table, adjusts the sleeves of her blazer, and sighs. "I'm not purposely manipulating JJ to get him to further our cause."

"But—"

"No buts," Charlie spits. "I'm not doing that to him. Mom, I love this man. I want a future with him. And setting him up to lose a job he's passionate about is not happening." Charlie peers down at me. "I'll be outside. Take your time."

Five minutes later, we're walking to Charlie's car when her phone rings.

"Speak of the devil." She taps the screen. "Hi, JJ." She halts in the middle of the parking garage and turns to me, eyes wide. "No problem," she tells him. "I understand. Tomorrow night, then?"

What, I'm wondering, is this about?

Seconds later, she hangs up, tucking her device in her purse. "One problem solved."

"What's that?"

"He just got called for the AG's advisory committee. When the Attorney General of the United States calls a meeting, you don't say no."

"What time is that?"

She clucks her tongue. "It's a dinner meeting that will probably run late. We're doing our evidence review tomorrow night."

Which means we're free tonight. Which means, Charlie doesn't have to sacrifice her body—not that sex with JJ is a sacrifice for her because she has trouble keeping her hands off him. She also doesn't need to manipulate him into allowing us access to Mary Hartman.

"Sooo," I say, rocking back on my heels. "I could go to this fundraiser. We'll leave you out of it. That way, you don't have to lie to JJ."

"No," Charlie replies and resumes walking.

I scramble after her. "Charlie, this is an opportunity. I mean, what are the chances he'll be called to a meeting on the very night we need him to be busy? If this isn't the universe throwing open a door, I don't know what is. We have to do this!"

"You're going whether I agree to accompany you or not, aren't you?"

"Yes."

My sister sighs as if I'm her burden to bear. "You could end up with Mom tonight."

"It'll be worth it if I can get something out of Mary."

She twists her mouth in thought. I'm almost sure she's about to budge off her high horse. She doesn't. "We do nothing until tomorrow. I want your word."

Her phone rings. I see her hesitation. "Who is it?"

"Unknown number." She's about to send it to voicemail.

"What if it's Mom using a cell she conned from a guard?"

"Or one she made a deal with an inmate for." She climbs into the driver's seat and hits the accept button, putting it on speaker. "Charlie Schock."

"Dr. Schock," a woman's shaky voice says. "My name is Mallory Rugers. I'm Gerald Hartman's ex. We don't know each other, but I was hoping to speak to you about my daughter's case."

Ms. Rugers has done her homework. No one calls Charlie by her title unless she's on the stand and the prosecution needs to impress the jury with her credentials.

"I'm sorry for the pain my family is causing yours," she says, not without genuine empathy, but apologizing has become a rote gesture for her today. "My mother can overstep common boundaries when it comes to finding justice. She's passionate."

"I'm so grateful for it," Mallory says.

Charlie glances at me, confused. "You are?"

"I've begged the family to keep pressing the police, but my demands have been shoved under the rug. Tiffany"—her voice hitches—"loved Christmas. Now, every year, I see blood instead of wrapping paper. The brutality of it. Have you seen the pictures? My precious baby, beaten to death at a family party."

Mallory could be a gold mine of information. Charlie senses this, too. "Would you be willing to come to our office and speak to us tomorrow?" she asks.

"I'm in France," Mallory says. "I can't stand to be anywhere near the Hartmans, especially during the holidays."

I pipe up. "What about a video chat?"

"My sister, Meg," Charlie says. "You're on speaker."

"If Mary found out..." Mallory trails off. "Let me think about it, all right? Just, please, dig into the case for me, will you? There's something not right about that family. I've always believed they know more than they've let on. Especially Mary. The matriarch of the Hartman clan knows everything. Every skeleton, every dirty secret."

"Does she have some kind of blackmail on you?" Charlie asks. "Is that why you're reluctant to talk to us?"

A soft chuckle that turns into a barely there sniffle. "She owns all of us."

"Owns you how?" I ask.

The line goes dead.

It's all I can do not to say something. To prod my sister. We have to attend that gala tonight and track down Mary Hartman.

Charlie starts the car and cranks up the heat. "I know what you're going to say."

I bite my lip. I know when to push and when to let Charlie's inner compass do it.

She drives out of the lot, and we hit the highway. I'm practically vibrating with the words backing up in my throat.

Finally, she says, "Fine. We're both going."

"What about—"

"JJ? I'll figure it out, Meg. I always do."

7

———

Charlie

The noise in the marble-floored foyer swallows our footsteps. Christmas joy is in the air, fueled by flowing liquor and vulture-like gossip.

My sister's plain black boots look blasphemous among the designer heels on every woman in sight. Her tailored slacks are an act of war among three-thousand-dollar gowns.

A woman in ice-blue satin recoils as Meg adjusts her favorite tote that's slung over her shoulder—the one carrying her sketchpad and latex gloves like her version of Santa's sack.

I straighten my Burberry trench, the lining too thin for the winter night. At least I'm wearing a Stella McCartney dress. Sure, it's *so last season*, as Haley pointed out, but gala events aren't generally high on my priority list. All I need to do is blend in.

I've made up for it by choosing some killer heels—no one can fault me there. They make me feel more confident. "I maxed out my last credit card on these tickets." The heels make me taller than her. "We better make this count."

"We should have brought Matt," she says.

"The two tickets for us were my limit."

Checking our coats, I stop long enough to reapply lipstick. Meg fusses with her white shirt. "You look great," I tell her.

She's left her hair down to frame her face and worn makeup that highlights her cheekbones. "Thanks. Now that I'm in here, maybe I should have worn a dress. My act of rebellion backfired. I look like one of the wait staff."

I wink. "The perfect undercover costume."

The ballroom is packed. Crystal chandeliers with teardrop pendants fracture light into dozens of rainbow shards that dance across the faces of the crowd. A string quartet plays Vivaldi while socialites dissect each other with diamond-studded smiles. I clock twelve security earpieces before we reach the ice sculpture centerpiece—swan wings melting into puddles at its base.

As a waiter with a tray waltzes past, Meg helps herself to canapes. The next tray-toting server brings champagne. I arch a brow as she downs the food and drink.

"I'm hungry," she says around a pastry tart.

At least she's eating.

"Remember our plan." I scan the nearest couple, but I need higher ground to locate our target. "No harassing. We get her alone and plead our case."

Meg grips my elbow. "Ten o'clock. Balcony."

Mary Hartman's presence at the top of the double staircase invokes images of a queen holding court. Her smile is pasted on as she converses with a group of admirers. Her jewelry screams old money, while her generous frame is stuffed artfully into a rich emerald green gown.

She makes some excuse and disappears from her entourage.

"Let's split up." I palm my phone, its screen lit with my list of questions for the woman. "You take the far staircase. I'll take this one. That way, we're sure to catch her. If anyone speaks to her, just keep an eye on her until she's free."

"Good luck." Meg vanishes into the sea of tuxedos and sequins. I weave my way past a drunk socialite doing a live video on her social media feed.

A silver-haired dowager steps into my path, her brooch glittering with enough carats to fund our office for a decade. "Darling," she quips, "Who let you in?" Her smile could fillet salmon.

I can't help it—I lie. "FBI, ma'am. Undercover. I'm on the hunt for a serial killer. Now, if you'll get out of my way...?"

Her veneer slips, and her lips flap before she asks, "Are we in danger?"

I lean in and lower my voice. "Only if I hit the fire alarm. Act normal otherwise."

On my way up the carpeted steps, I pass hedge fund wives clutching pearls and heir apparents comparing Rolexes. Camera flashes erupt near a towering spruce strung with hand-blown ornaments.

A man downing Manhattans tries to grab my ass. I step on one of his Gucci loafers, and he backs away.

Then I see her—platinum updo, razor-cut cheekbones, vermilion nails. Mary Hartman, backlit by the Christmas tree like a Bond villain.

She's holding court next to the second-floor Christmas tree, her gown reflecting light.

Six paces. Four.

Three women hover around her—a Prada-Dior-Versace human shield. One snaps her fingers at a server. "More Krug. Vintage."

The teenage server in an ill-fitting tux rushes off to retrieve the champagne.

Wait for Meg, I remind myself. *Stick to the plan.*

I loiter in the tree's shadow, admiring the icicle ornaments. Dagger-shaped. Decorative. Potentially deadly.

Down below, the quartet switches songs. Prada, Dior, and Versace continue to hang on Mary's every word. I text Meg. *Where are you?*

Some guy spilled champagne on me. Did you find her?

Yes. Hurry.

A man joins the group—likely Ms. Prada's husband. They argue quietly. Mary cuts them off. "Take it somewhere else."

Dior and Versace make a quick exit. My chance. I can't wait for Meg. I step out from the shadows. "Mrs. Hartman?"

Her neck shifts, a predatory calculation behind the movement. Not enough to acknowledge, just enough to inspect.

"Charlize Schock." I offer my card. "Schock Investigations. I wanted to apologize—"

Her fingers tighten on her flute. A single diamond teardrop earring sways. "Why are you here?"

"Supporting a wonderful cause," I say smoothly. "I saw you and wanted to express my regret at the spectacle my mother has made, but if you'd consider discussing the case with us, we'd be happy to offer our services pro bono. Your family deserves peace."

Champagne flutes clink in the background. The hum of so many conversations nearly drowns out the quartet's music. Mary pivots but barely raises her voice. "You mistake me for someone who tolerates scavengers at my events."

I stash my card since she's not interested in remaining professional. I consider different tactics I learned from my Quantico interrogations. "Meg and I are good at our jobs. We unearth the truth instead of bodies. Isn't that what we all want?"

Her laugh could frost the windows. "Do you bill by the cliché or the hour?"

A server edges closer. I consider grabbing a flute, but Mary gives him a scowl that sends him scurrying off. I hold onto my patience. "I assure you, I'm only interested in putting a killer behind bars."

"You're a vulture who confuses her hero complex with entertainment."

Ouch.

Someone gasps. I glance around to find we have an audience. Phones emerge like weapons drawn.

JJ is going to kill me. Bury me where no one can find my body.

"Leave." Mary's voice rises, as does her chin. She's playing for the cameras now. "Before I have you arrested for harassment."

"Arrest me." I let the words ride the room. "I'm only trying to uncover the truth. It seems to me that if you were interested in that, you'd be more than happy for the Schock Sisters to take on this case." Mary isn't the only one who can play to the cameras, although I'm partial to my mother's more straightforward, less drama-queen style. "As I said, we're good at our job, and I'm offering to do it free of charge. What do you have to lose?"

Murmurs. Nods.

Her mask slips. "Filthy little climber. You're here to spotlight my grief and leverage my standing in this community. Your mother's obsession is tragic. Don't be like her." Her voice rises. "Helen Schock couldn't distinguish real journalism from hysterical fanfiction if a serial killer walked up and confessed every secret he had."

"My mother has brought closure to multiple families. Her heart is in the right place."

A champagne flute shatters.

Alex Hartman barrels through the crowd, tuxedo perfect,

fury barely contained. He plants himself between Mary and the cameras. "What are you doing, Charlie?"

Mary grips his sleeve and turns pleading eyes on him. "This gutter snipe is harassing me. I told the mayor I wanted protection from the Schocks, and she shows up anyway, trying to ruin everything." Her bottom lip wobbles, and her voice cracks.

Oh, she's good.

Alex's gaze locks on mine. "I said I'd help you, but you had to leave my mother out of it. JJ told you she was off limits. Congratulations, you've just made me your enemy."

The ballroom tilts. I steady my breathing. My voice drops to glacial. "I'm not afraid of you or your mother. But if anyone in your family is hiding something, you should be afraid of me. Because if I find anything, I will take it to the world. I will find Tiffany's murderer and bring him"—I glance at Mary—"or her, to justice."

A muscle ticks in his jaw. "Leave. Or I call security."

I count three heartbeats. Five. Let the silence stretch until the guests begin murmuring. Then I smile—wide and bright for the audience. "Enjoy your night, Mrs. Hartman."

I walk away. Slowly. Deliberately. A hundred cameras on me.

By the coat check, I finally unclench my fists and text Meg to tell her to meet me there. Four half-moon wounds glisten on my left palm.

Already? she replies. *Did you get the dirt?*

I start to type something, delete it. JJ is going to hate me. My mother will be disappointed. *Crashed and burned.* Wait 'til she sees the footage on social media. *It was spectacular.*

Good for you. Hitting the bathroom. Meet you in the lobby.

Grabbing our coats, I start composing my apology to JJ in my head. I'm going to need it. And wine.

Lots of wine.

8

——————

Meg

Sticking to the outer wall of the ballroom, I bypass the throngs of people—and the overwhelming mass of energy that comes with them—and head to the last set of double doors in search of the bathroom.

It's not hot in here, but I feel a furnace blast inside me and sweat beads on my upper lip. It all feels...close. Stuffy.

Suffice it to say, these are not my people.

In many ways. I'm too ... hippy. Too casual in appearance, which, yes, maybe my act of rebellion in wearing slacks was ill-advised. But at the time, I thought it was a grand way of letting the filthy rich know I don't need glittering gowns and jewelry to substantiate my worth.

Now, I see how I've more than likely insulted the uber-rich sequestered in this ballroom and brought unwanted attention to myself.

Lesson learned for next time.

Shaking my head over my misstep, I yearn for the quiet of my office. My studio and art and the victims who need our help.

That's what I should be focused on.

In the hallway, I glance right, see no signs for a ladies' room, and then turn left. Barely twenty feet away, I hit pay dirt.

The champagne I downed too fast gave me a buzz despite the appetizers I inhaled. Champagne has never been my friend.

Still, I don't mind the effect. It's sort of how I feel about weed. It allows me to let go of … well…everything.

Including the reconstructions—so many reconstructions—of murder victims who've been tossed away like trash.

We can't solve them all.

That's what Charlie likes to say.

Maybe not, but we can try.

Champagne.

Once again, I shake my head, trying to organize my scattered thoughts as I push through the ladies' room door and find the first empty stall.

While I'm taking care of business, a blast of voices sounds as two women enter the bathroom. They're not right in front of the stalls, though. It sounds farther. Maybe from the sitting area just beyond the wall of sinks.

"Mother," a woman says, "why are you walking away from me?"

"Perhaps, dear, because my lipstick needs a touch-up and I don't want to talk about this?"

The second woman sounds older. More haughty and high-brow, and I instantly recoil.

Not my people.

"Obviously," the daughter responds. "Which baffles me. You're the one always prodding me for donations for the auction."

One of the toilets flushes while I finish my own business and stand to put myself back together.

"Can you blame me?" The conversation continues. "You work for a designer. Seems to me, you would have excellent contacts."

"Yes. And they've donated. Plenty. The shoes Andre gave retail for $5,000."

"And I'm grateful."

"You're also dodging the question."

"Forgive me. What was the question, again?"

"The bag!" The daughter hisses.

"Lower your voice," the older woman says.

Outside the stall, the other occupant washes her hands, and through the crack in the door, I spot her walking by. A second later, more noise erupts from the hallway, and then the room goes quiet again.

"We talked about this weeks ago," the younger woman says. "You're sitting on a Sherman that's vintage. Thirty years old. Its value has skyrocketed in the last two years. One fetched $25,000 at an auction last month. Yours is a never used vintage. I don't have to tell you, of all people, what that kind of money could do for the Hartman Foundation."

Whoa.

These women are involved with the Hartmans. Could they *be* the Hartmans?

Unable to put it off any longer, I smack the toilet handle, flush, and open the stall door. The two women stand just beyond the sinks near the sitting area and...

Yep.

Mary Hartman has her back to me while talking to a tall blonde in a glittering royal blue gown. Must be Alex's sister. What was her name?

Damned champagne. I do my trick of visualizing my mother's research. The list of names at the holiday party.

Christina. Yes. Six years older than Alex and following in her mother's footsteps as a social dynamo. Rumor has it that Christina's claws and acerbic tongue are nearly as dangerous as her mother's.

Holy, holy cow.

I wave my hand under the faucet, and a paltry flow dribbles out. Taking my time, I soap up.

"Christina, it's my bag. It was a Christmas gift. You know that. And I would think you know..." Mary catches herself. "Suffice it to say, I'm hesitant to give it up."

"Actually, I'd think, given the circumstances of that Christmas, you'd want nothing more than to give it up."

"Listen to me," Mary says, the steel in her voice cold enough to send a shiver through me despite the warm water. "I'm not having this conversation with you. I'll write the foundation a check for $25,000 if it'll make you happy."

Unable to prolong washing my hands—I mean, even the biggest germaphobe eventually has to stop—I grab a paper towel from the stack on the sink. And, hello? They should really switch to automatic dryers and save a few trees.

On my way to the door, Christina eyes me over her mother's shoulder. Her eyes lock on mine for a brief second, and Mary begins to turn. Before she can see my face, I hustle behind her, giving her my back as I slip out. The door shuts behind me, the whoosh echoing in my ears.

Did Mary see me? Even if she did, there's no way—I don't think—she would know me. Unless she's researched Mom, which, considering Helen Schock's use of social media these days, is not a stretch.

All I know for sure is I have no interest in hanging around. Moving at a clip, I hightail it down the corridor, cutting around the random guests milling about.

A minute later, I enter the lobby and find Charlie scrolling through her phone.

"Hey," I say, the word coming out too breathy.

Apparently, I need to start exercising if I'm this winded from such a short walk.

Disregarding her phone, Charlie peers up at me and hands me my coat. "Hi. All set?"

I quickly slip it on. "Yes. But," I swing a look over my shoulder, making sure I wasn't followed before I grab my sister's arm.

"Meg, what is it?"

"Outside," I mutter.

I drag her to the exit and push through. A blast of cold wind assails me, and I hold my coat closed with one hand.

On the sidewalk, Charlie passes the ticket to the valet, and I survey the area. Given the early hour, we're the only ones waiting for a car, but a couple dressed in layers and hunched against the cold moves by us, heading into the lobby.

After they're out of earshot, I lower my voice. "Mary Hartman and her daughter were in the bathroom."

Charlie angles back, meeting my gaze with that hard, touch-my-sister-and-I'll-kill-you stare. "What happened? Did she say something to you?"

I shake my head. "Her back was to me. I overheard them talking. Something about a vintage Sherman bag. I have no idea what that is."

"It's a purse," Charlie says. "Polly Sherman, the former first lady, had it designed when she couldn't find one with enough pockets. They're handmade and used to be leather, but now they're vegan. The leather ones are rare. And expensive."

"Well," I say, "Christina, Mary's daughter, wanted her to auction hers. Mary apparently didn't agree. From what I heard, Mary got the bag as a gift. A Christmas gift. Thirty years ago."

An eyebrow quirk. "Huh."

Thoughts rattle around in my brain, trying to latch on to... something. I don't know what it is, but my Spidey-Sense is on high alert. "Christina said something about how, given the circumstances, Mary should want to get rid of it. I'm assuming she means because she got it the Christmas Tiffany was killed. Could the bag be connected somehow?"

Charlie narrows her eyes. "Anything is possible. Particularly if Mary wants to keep it quiet."

"Something is weird with this bag," I say.

"When you were reading Mom's files, did you see anything about a Sherman? I know a lot of the items, including the gifts, were taken into evidence that night. Most, if not all, were returned."

"I don't remember seeing anything about a purse. But I wasn't necessarily looking for it."

"Huh," Charlie says again.

"What?"

She peers at me with blank eyes. "I don't know. But the Sherman has me wondering. What if Tiffany wasn't the target? Could the bag have something to do with someone else being the target?"

Yikes. "Could be, I suppose."

"Ma'am?"

The male voice draws me from my raging thoughts. We both turn to where the valet stands beside Charlie's car, holding up the key.

"Sorry," she calls, then comes back to me. "We're going back to the office."

"Why?"

She steps around me. "Because Mom's notes are there and we need to see if there's anything about a Sherman bag."

9

______

Charlie

Meg bursts into laughter as we enter the back door of Schock Investigations. "You actually told Mary and Alex that you're coming for them?"

I drop my bag onto Haley's desk as I flip on lights and turn up the heat. I'm freezing. I blame it on the cold night, but the realization of what's going to happen when JJ finds out about me confronting Mary is the actual reason. "Not in so many words, but...sort of?"

"Charlie Schock, you are terrible. Good, but terrible."

I follow her to her workroom. "Let's find that evidence list."

She slips out of her coat, points to the battered box. "There are dozens of pages of it in there."

I haul it to the conference room, and we spread the documents across the table like a jigsaw puzzle: police photographs, witness statements, property inventory forms—each piece representing fragments of the terrible night that ended Tiffany's life.

"Here's the first list." Meg flips through a stack of sheets and passes me a second stapled set. "I don't remember seeing the purse, but if Mary received it as a gift that night, it should be here, correct?"

"Not necessarily." I trace down a column of items. "We don't know for sure that she received it then, or that the police confiscated it."

After a minute, Meg sighs. "Not a single note about a Sherman bag in my list. Maybe you're right—maybe she got it as a gift on a different Christmas. Or another night? I wish I'd gotten more info about it."

My phone buzzes. I glance at the screen, and my stomach drops.

"JJ?" Meg asks, reading my expression.

I nod and show her his text: *We need to talk. I'm on my way.*

"It was inevitable." I consider responding that I'm going to bed, but he traces my phone, so he knows I'm here.

It annoys me, his constant vigilance, yet after the scrapes Meg and I have been in, I understand his reasons for it. He thinks I don't know about the tracer, and if I get pissed enough, I'll use his overstepping male protectiveness to threaten his balls.

Meg's eyes meet mine with her usual empathy. It makes me remember why I'm glad she's my sister. "He's already heard about the gala?"

"I'm sure Alex called him." I toss the phone aside. "There was quite a bit of social media coverage of the exchange. Lots of photos and videos. We need something concrete before JJ gets here. Speaking of photos." I sit up as an idea strikes. "Are there any pictures in these boxes of the party before the crime took place? You know, family shots in front of the tree? Drunken partygoers toasting the camera? That sort of thing?"

"That was before people documented everything on every social media platform available," Meg says. "But maybe."

For ten tense minutes, we toil in silence, going through all the boxes. Finally, I slam down a hand in exasperation. "Nothing. Not a single mention of a Sherman bag and no photos of Mary showing it off."

"Again, your assumption could be right," Meg says. "Maybe the bag wasn't part of that night's gift-giving after all."

I stare at the scattered papers, defeat eating at me. Another idea hits. Scrolling through my calls, I tap Mallory's number.

"Who are you calling?" Meg asks.

Tiffany's mother picks up on the second ring, and I put her on speaker. "Ms. Rugers, it's Charlize Schock. I'm sorry to bother you so late, but—"

"Did you find something?" Mallory asks without preamble. There's a trace of hope in her voice.

"Not exactly. Do you remember if Mary received a Sherman bag as a gift the night Tiffany died?"

Mallory pauses as if scanning her memories. "Phillip gave her one—a limited sort of thing. Mary couldn't stop showing it off all evening, flaunting it like a trophy."

Phillip, Mary's husband. The man's been dead for twenty-some years. "Did you ever see the bag after that night?"

Another pause as she thinks it over. "No, I don't think so. Why? Is it important?"

"Just following up on a few details," I tell her. Once I assure her that I'll be in touch if I have any other questions or breakthroughs, I disconnect.

Meg is grinning. "So, it does exist, and Mary got it that Christmas Eve."

"And it's disappeared, just like the murder weapon." It's circumstantial, but my gut gives a kick. "Did someone deliberately keep it out of the evidence log? Was it not there for them to take? Or did the detective in charge then not think it was important?" My brain churns. "Mary might have hidden it to make sure it wasn't taken simply because she didn't want to lose her new purse, or the crime scene investigators may have deemed it irrelevant to the murder."

"They sure didn't deem anything else irrelevant." Meg flips through the pages of her evidence log. "They confiscated tools belonging to the construction workers, candlestick holders, statues, Christmas decorations, toys...pretty much anything and everything that Tiffany might have touched or been around. They even took the bar cart."

The familiar chime of the front door brings both of us to attention. JJ doesn't announce his arrival—the sheer confident stride of his footsteps in the hallway does that for him.

"Charlie," Meg says with a tone that reminds me of Mom. "Whatever happens, we're in this together."

JJ might be the Emperor of Cold Cases with his perfect suits and storm-cloud eyes, but he's about to meet the stubborn determination that makes the Schock sisters a force to be reckoned with. I'm not backing down. Neither is Meg.

He fills the doorway in an impeccable Armani suit, unable to hide the tension in his broad shoulders. His usual easy smile is nowhere in sight; instead, a tight-lipped glare has replaced it. Those pretty eyes, which typically soften when they meet mine, hold the cold precision of a prosecutor on the hunt.

He doesn't bother with pleasantries. I expect him to yell; he doesn't. His voice comes out low and controlled. "What the hell were you thinking?"

Meg shifts uneasily. I meet JJ's gaze, even as the disappointment in his tone stings more than his anger ever could. "I ran into Mary at the gala and asked her a few questions," I say, striving to steady my voice. "She was flippant and dismissive."

"You threatened her and Alex. She has witnesses."

"Technically, I didn't threaten anyone. I apologized about Mom's antics and offered our services pro bono. She proceeded to insult me and Mom, and then *she* threatened *me*. Said she would have me thrown out of the gala, even though all I did was offer to look into Tiffany's case. An overreaction, don't you think?" I tap on one of the mountains of files before us. "Meg overheard her and her daughter talking about a designer bag that went missing the night of the murder. It wasn't logged as evidence, but Tiffany's mother confirmed Mary received it that night as a gift. It's a slim lead, but at least it's something."

JJ's jaw tightens. A muscle twitches under his five o'clock shadow. Silence stretches.

I press on. "The bag wasn't just any accessory." I pull up a photo of one—only a few are for sale on vintage websites. "It's big enough to conceal a murder weapon. Which, I might remind you, is also missing."

JJ doesn't even glance at the photo. "Stop."

That single word is an anvil falling.

He plants both palms on the table and leans toward me, visibly weary. "The mayor called. *Again*." His next words are measured like a sentence in a court ruling. "The Hartman case is closed, effective immediately. Put everything back in those boxes. I'm taking them with me."

My breath catches. "You can't be serious."

"You can't do that," Meg says. "Mom got all of this through the FOIA Act—"

"I'm aware of what the Act covers, and its exemptions," he snaps. "Are you?" He begins reciting it. "*Certain categories of documents may be withheld from disclosure. Included among these are documents that relate to law-enforcement activities, documents subject to recognized legal privileges such as the attorney-client and work-product privileges, documents required to be withheld by other laws, federal or District, documents that reflect the internal deliberative processes of the government, and documents the disclosure of which would result in a clearly unwarranted intrusion on personal privacy.*"

Meg pushes her chair back with a screech, jumping up and waving her hands. "That's bullshit, and you know it. Since when does the mayor decide how the U.S. Attorney's office handles a homicide investigation?"

His eyes narrow. His posture shifts into full courtroom predator. "Since always." His voice drops to a threatening undertone. "Especially since your sister compromised what little leeway this investigation had by harassing Mary at her own charity function."

Meg opens her mouth to protest, but a single look from him silences her. She sits.

"This isn't a negotiation." He straightens his tie, a gesture that reminds us this is business. He locks eyes with me. "It's over."

The statement suggests something more than just our investigation.

My body turns ice cold.

I've seen JJ confident, playful, even ferocious in the courtroom, but never like this, not with me.

I say nothing. He runs a hand through his dark hair, and for an instant, I catch a glimpse of the man I've grown to love. "My association with you has become...problematic."

The room tilts. I grip the edge of the table. "What?"

"The mayor and my boss believe my objectivity is compromised, and therefore, my perspective on investigations is as well. Because of you."

The air rushes out of me. "Because of *me*?"

He draws a breath and slowly lets it out through his nose. "I can't be seen fraternizing with a PI who's stirring up trouble in a politically sensitive investigation."

My heart plummets, leaving me speechless. I'm not sure my legs will hold me, but I stand anyway. "What exactly are you saying?"

"Are you breaking up with her?" Meg demands, also coming to her feet.

He says nothing. An answer in itself.

"So that's it?" I ask, forcing steadiness into my voice. This escalated quickly. Too quickly. "Your career's more important than the truth?" *Than me?*

"It's not that simple, Charlie."

"Isn't it? There are inconsistencies with this case, and the bigwigs are nervous because Mary is upset about our investigation. Since when does a civilian, who may herself be the murderer, get to call the shots on a case? What if that bag is connected? We're on to something. I can feel it."

"Feelings don't hold up in court," JJ replies, his jaw set. "And Mary is not a suspect. Detective Loren looked into her and everyone else at the party. None had motive."

"Someone at that party murdered that girl." I'm practically yelling. "I don't care what Loren or anyone else says. Mary Hartman is far too defensive about this for her to be innocent." I pull out all the stops. "Your instincts have led you to reopen cold cases that everyone else has written off," I remind him. "Trust mine and Meg's now. Please."

"Please," Meg echoes. "Seriously, JJ. I've never been more certain of anything. Mary's involved in this."

For a heartbeat, conflict flashes across his face, and I see *my* JJ. The one who cross-examines me over takeout while dissecting case files, the one who challenges my theories and respects my rebuttals.

Then it vanishes, replaced by the impassive mask of Joseph Jefferson Carrington III, U.S. Attorney. "I can't," he says, adjusting his cufflinks. All business again. "I won't jeopardize my job based on hunches and missing handbags."

The space between us cracks open into an unbearable chasm, separating our professional and personal lives. I suspected this moment might come someday, yet its reality is like a sucker punch.

"So where does that leave us?" My voice betrays the vulnerability swallowing me up.

"It leaves us exactly where we are," he says. "On opposite sides of a closed case. I've always thought I could trust you. That we were on the same page. Now?" He strides to the door without answering the question. He doesn't have to. He tries to hide the hurt in his voice, but I still hear it. I agreed to stay away from Mary, and I didn't. I broke his trust. "You can drop off those boxes at my office tomorrow."

I watch him leave, the words I want to call out locked in my throat. Meg grasps my hand, and it spurs me into action. I'm not going down without a fight. Not for the case—for us.

I chase him down the hall. "I thought you were different. That you respected me and my work."

He pauses, his profile sharp against the glow of the reception area's light. For one suspended moment, I think he might turn back and embrace me, but he only glances over his shoulder. "I thought the same about you."

As he exits, I stand rooted in place, staring at the spot where he stood, my mind whirling with a thousand scenarios—what I should have said, what I could have done, whether anything would have changed his mind.

"Charlie?" Meg's voice breaks through my spiraling thoughts as she comes up next to me. "You okay?"

I blink, forcing hot tears away. "No." She guides me back to the conference room. I slump into a chair. "But I guess feelings don't matter."

"They do matter." She pulls up a chair beside me. Her eyes, so reminiscent of mine, search my face. "He's out of line and a bastard for choosing his job over you."

"His job means everything to him."

"He's a fool, then."

I accept her hug, a few tears slipping down my face. "What am I going to do?"

"This isn't over. I'll go through everything tonight and have Matt take the boxes to JJ's office tomorrow. We keep going, regardless of what JJ and the mayor want. In the end, when we solve this thing, they'll be sorry."

She wants to take my mind off JJ's betrayal and get me to focus on something I can control. Classic Meg. Next, she'll offer me some of her gummy bears or a pot brownie. Maybe I need one. "Without the bag, without official backing, without—"

"Without fear of stepping on official toes," she finishes. "We never needed permission before to solve a cold case, and we don't now. Mary Hartman's expensive accessory disappeared that night for a reason. It has to be connected to the murder. I'm sure of it."

Her phone buzzes loudly across the table, displaying Jerome's name and a photo of him playing his guitar. Meg's eyes flick from it to me, her hand hovering indecisively before she deliberately turns the screen face down.

At least this is something that can distract me from my damning feelings. "Everything okay?"

Her fingers drum on the table. "It's complicated."

I raise an eyebrow, studying the unusual flicker of uncertainty on her face. "When isn't it with you two? What's going on?"

She tugs a strand of hair, twisting it around her finger. A debate rages behind her eyes. "We should focus on you and JJ."

Another classic Meg move—deflect with a redirection worthy of a magician's assistant. I wiggle my fingers at her. "Spill."

She huffs loudly, grabbing a pencil to doodle on a notepad. Once, twice, three times around a circle, each rotation digging deeper into the paper. "Jerome asked me to marry him two days ago."

The words hang between us, and I try to process them. Perfect. A fresh wound and now a surprise proposal bomb. Better to focus on Meg rather than JJ. "As in...marriage? Jerome Metcalfe? The guy who showed up to my birthday dinner wearing two different shoes?"

"That's him," she confirms with a slight grin that lights up her face, then fades like the last sparks of a firecracker. "He's been different lately. More serious."

I've noticed a few changes—Jerome with his honey-blond hair neatly tied back, his clean-shaven face, his presence more adult-like. A far cry from the disheveled artist who floats through Meg's life, trailing the scent of marijuana and creative chaos.

"What prompted this?" I ask.

"The music store offered him an assistant manager position. He's showing me dozens of fixer-uppers and condos." Meg laughs, a hint of hysteria in it. "Can you believe it? Jerome, who once lived in his van for six months because he 'forgot' to pay rent, wants to buy real estate. And he wants me to be his wife."

Her phone buzzes again, and we both watch it vibrate on the table. "You haven't said yes?"

She gestures helplessly. "I panicked and said I needed time to think. I've been dodging his calls since."

"But you love him." Not that that's a reason to get married, but it sure helps.

She stares at the ceiling and fiddles with her pencil. "Honestly, part of me believes it could work. He makes me laugh. He sees the world in colors I never notice. But marriage? Jerome can barely commit to a simple breakfast order."

"What scares you more?" I ask softly. "That he's not ready, or that *you're* not?"

She jams the end of the pencil into the pad. "I...I don't know if I'm built for that life, Charlie. This whole settle-down thing.

What if, in five years, I wake up feeling suffocated? Or what if he does?"

"There are no guarantees, but I've seen the way you look at him when you think nobody's watching. Why does it have to be marriage? What if you just try living together?"

"I don't know. This whole thing confuses me." She chuckles. "God, listen to me. Your relationship with JJ just collapsed, and here I am, whining over commitment."

"Hey," I say firmly, "my romantic disaster doesn't invalidate what's going on with you. We're both allowed to be messy sometimes."

That draws a genuine laugh. "The Schock sisters—screwing up their professional and private lives in one fell swoop."

"Whatever you decide with Jerome, I'm in your corner. Even if it means helping you escape out a bathroom window on your wedding day."

Her smile wavers. "You'd do that for me?"

"I'll bring the getaway car and snacks."

The files lay scattered around us, briefly forgotten reminders of official restraints now closing in on our investigation. Yet, in that moment of sisterly support, those obstacles feel less insurmountable.

Still, JJ's order has become a ticking clock. I gather a pile of papers to start running through our copier, the FOIA rules be damned. "Mallory's confirmation is huge."

Meg rolls up the sleeves of her white shirt, sorting through photos with habitual precision. "This could be the lead we need."

I tap my finger against my bottom lip. "We need to trace the bag's journey. Who might have seen it after the murder?"

Meg's eyes light up. "What about the event staff? Catering, the cleanup crew—someone might have noticed it."

"Good thinking," I agree, thumbing through a file until I locate the list of service personnel. "I can have Haley track these people down tomorrow. Seeing as how it was thirty years ago, it's a long shot, but it's better than nothing."

"Do you think the murder was planned or a spur-of-the-moment thing?" Meg asks.

"Premeditation points to someone at the event, not a random break-in gone wrong, but it could still be a random act. Someone got mad at the girl, a game got out of hand. Might have even been an accident."

"Whatever happened, it's been covered up. What if Mary had already sold off the bag or pawned it?" Meg asks. "I think we should talk to the daughter. I can do it—she doesn't know who I am. I can say I overheard her talking about it, and I've always wanted one."

"Nah. That's a job for Matt and his pretty blue eyes. I'll sic him on the woman tomorrow and let him come up with some story to get her to tell him about it."

Before we can continue brainstorming, my phone rings. I snatch it up, half hoping it's JJ calling to apologize. It isn't.

"Charlie, hey. It's Alex Hartman."

My brows shoot to my hairline. I put the call on speaker for Meg. "Alex. This is... unexpected."

"I want to apologize for my reaction at the gala." His voice is stripped of its earlier arrogance. "I was out of line."

Meg's expression mirrors my surprise.

"I thought about what you said," he continues. "About Tiffany deserving justice, regardless of political fallout. My mother believes you're doing it for the notoriety. I know better. I want..." He clears his throat. "I want to help. I might have some useful connections that could prove beneficial."

"I'm sorry," I say. "We've been officially ordered off the case."

"I know." He doesn't sound daunted. "Which is why I thought you could use an ally who knows all about the family and our friends. One who was there that night. I was only nine, but some of those folks are still around."

I can't believe our luck. It's too lucky. Time to test his loyalties—with his family, his job, and especially his mother. "We're trying to track down any clue that could lead us to a missing Sherman bag your mother received as a gift that Christmas Eve. Do you remember it?"

"Uh...no. Like I said, I was nine. Purses weren't of interest to me."

"Are you up for helping us locate it?"

The slightest hesitation. "How about I come by tomorrow, say around eight-thirty? You can tell me everything you know so far, and I'll see what I can do to answer your questions."

JJ might have closed the official investigation, but he forgot one crucial thing: I never leave a puzzle unsolved. And now, with an unexpected ally on the inside, we might just be able to reopen this case on our terms.

10

Meg

After barely five hours sleep, I'm back at the office by seven-thirty, standing over the world's slowest coffee pot.

Or maybe I'm just impatient.

Irritable.

Nothing about this case has gone right. Mom in jail, JJ dumping Charlie, zero solid leads. All of it adds up to us spinning our wheels on the murder of a child.

My stomach shrivels. *Damned cold cases.*

Finally, the pot gurgles, alerting the masses—meaning me —that it's done.

Mug at the ready, I pour, toss some Stevia in, and head to the conference room.

Last night, Charlie and I sorted through files, organizing them into neat piles. Now, I'm overwhelmed by the stacks littering a table that seats ten.

I inhale, hold it for five seconds.

I need a starting place. *Just one.*

Suspects.

Excellent.

I move to the giant whiteboard on the far wall, uncap a marker, and write the suspects in all caps. Below that, I add Mary's name.

For a few seconds, I stare at it, then add: Regal. Controlled.

Of the hundreds at that party, Mary knew every inch of that estate. And had access to every person.

Not all in attendance would be suspects, but even so, any of them could be involved.

I stick to the immediate family and add Mallory's name, and then Tiffany's father, Gerald. Nothing about Mallory killing her daughter makes sense. Still, we can't rule her out yet. Tiffany was an only child, so I continue by grabbing Mom's list of potential suspects and include aunts, uncles, and cousins.

By the time I'm done, I have twenty-five. There are more family members, but I've started with first cousins and will see where that takes us.

We can build on these names. Draw conclusions and make connections that might help us identify more suspects.

It's a start.

I draw a line down the center and write MURDER WEAPON.

The autopsy report indicates Tiffany suffered blunt force trauma to the right temporal region. The weapon was never found but given the shape of the wounds and the fact that the safe room was under construction, a hammer could have been used.

I add HAMMER and wander back to the stacks on the table searching for the evidence lists. I skim the pages for at least the tenth time since last evening.

Nope.

Not a hammer to be found.

Remembering my now nearly cold coffee, I take a swig, hopeful the caffeine will jump-start my brain.

A chime sounds, alerting me that the rear door has been opened. My sister, eyes puffy and shadowed, appears.

"Morning," she says.

"Hi." I hold up my mug. "Coffee is on."

"Good. Matt is five minutes out."

I nod. "Okay. Maybe fresh eyes will help us out here because we have zip. What's happening with Mom?"

"The lawyer I hired called. Her arraignment is at nine. Dad is arranging bail."

Our poor father. The man is destined for sainthood. "I contacted him this morning."

"Me too," Charlie says. "He sounds…"

"Broken?"

It suddenly hits me that the Schocks are dealing with all sorts of relationship drama. Charlie got dumped, I'm terrified of a marriage proposal, and Dad is dealing with…well…Mom.

"Yes," Charlie says. "Good word for it."

"He's exhausted," I say. "Of all mom's antics, I wouldn't be surprised if this one puts him over the edge."

My sister cocks her head, stares at me for a solid ten seconds. "You don't think he'd leave her. Do you?"

I shrug. JJ just left her. And she didn't do anything nearly as humiliating.

"I'm tired," I say. "Everything feels like a catastrophe."

Charlie nods. "I hear you. Let me take off my coat and get some coffee. Be right back."

Ten minutes later, Charlie, Matt, and I sit at the table. My sister is directly across from me, with Matt to her right. He rocks back, placing his hands on top of his head.

"You've got Gerald on the board. His brother, Phillip, was Mary's husband, right?"

"Yes. Gerald was the rich party boy spending the family's fortune while Phillip was the responsible one."

"What do we know about him?"

Charlie grabs a small stack and rifles through it. "I saw something in here last evening. He was interviewed that night. Claimed he didn't know anything and barely noticed Tiffany at the party."

More rifling ensues until Charlie finally holds up a stapled report. "Here it is. The detectives did a deep dive on him. He was quite the drinker. Mary and the kids wouldn't comment, but a cousin who worked with Phillip claimed the pressure of being the Hartman patriarch—and covering for Gerald's behavior—was getting to him."

"And Phillip is where?" Matt asks.

"Deceased," Charlie says. "A year after Tiffany's death, he dropped dead of a heart attack during a meeting."

Interesting.

Or is it?

I mean, with the combined stress of running an empire, a pain-in-the-ass brother whose child had been murdered, and the ensuing media attention on their typically very private family might be enough to give anyone a stress-induced cardiac event.

Matt lowers his hands and sits forward, pointing at the report still in Charlie's hand. "Anything in there about Gerald and Phillip's relationship? Aside from Phil being frustrated. Were they on the outs?"

Charlie skims the report. "There's nothing."

"Let's call Mallory," I say. "She's the only Hartman—"

"Former Hartman," Charlie says.

"Former Hartman willing to help us. It's afternoon in Paris. Maybe she'll pick up."

Charlie grabs a legal pad and pen from the middle of the table and sets them in front of her before dialing. She taps the screen, and the room fills with the sound of a ringing line.

"Hi, Charlie," Mallory says.

"Hey, I'm sorry to bother you."

"It's no bother. I'm grateful someone is trying to find my daughter's killer. What can I do for you?"

"I have Meg and Matt, our investigator, here. We're reviewing evidence files in the case. There's nothing about the relationship between Phillip and Gerald. We're hoping you can give us a sense of it. Did they get along?"

"Eh," she says. "They didn't *not* get along. It was weird."

"Weird how?" I ask.

"Phillip would lecture Gerry about his carousing. The man was a pig. Women, drinking, drugs. It never stopped. It's why I divorced him. He'd blow through his monthly allowance and then have to call Phillip for funds. Gerry found it demoralizing to have to ask when it was his trust, but Phillip was the custodian."

"Did he ever deny the money?"

"Never, but he didn't make it easy on Gerry. Mary didn't like Gerry, and there was underlying tension between them, but Phillip did his best to get Gerry help. Not that it worked."

Charlie jots some notes. "You mentioned Gerald found it demoralizing to ask for money. Did he ever talk to Phillip about that?"

"Not that I know of. And, I don't think he would have. I don't keep in touch with him, but I've heard he's as wild as ever. He's never had a job, and he needs the Hartman money, so he won't make waves. Even when it comes to his daughter's murder."

I snap my gaze to Charlie. That last sentence was delivered with a sharp enough edge that my sister's eyebrows have hiked up.

"What do you mean?" she asks.

"For years, I begged him to throw the Hartman name around to see if we could get some help on the case. They ask for political favors all the time. I didn't think it was too much to ask for help with Tiffany. But he refused."

My jaw drops. What an asshole.

"He claimed," Mallory continues, "it wouldn't be appropriate. Which translates to, he couldn't afford to create issues in the family because he needed the money. He sacrificed his child for wealth. I finally gave up and haven't spoken to him in nearly fifteen years. I despise that man."

Yikes.

I think of the little girl who wanted to be a hairstylist. Her father prevented her from getting justice so he could stay wealthy.

Charlie flips a page and jots a note, holding it up to Matt and me. Any more questions?

I shake my head, and so does Matt.

"Okay. This helps. Thank you, Mallory. We'll keep you posted."

Charlie disconnects. "So, Gerald is a scumbag of the highest degree, but that doesn't make him a killer of his own child."

"Agreed," I say.

"Yeah," Matt adds. "I'm not seeing it."

The sound of our front doorbell sounds. Haley hasn't arrived yet, and we no longer keep our doors unlocked for any psycho to walk in on us.

Charlie picks up her phone and pokes the screen. No doubt checking the security app.

"It's Alex."

I check the clock on the credenza. Eight-ten. "He's early."

"Fine by me." Charlie stands and heads to the door. "We can ask him about his father."

Once Charlie is gone, I peer at Matt. "Should we erase the board? I can take a picture and redo it."

For a few seconds, he simply stares at it in that distant way he does when contemplating a serious situation.

"No," he says. "Let him see his name up there. Maybe it'll rattle him."

If this were an average family we were dealing with, I'd buy into this line of thinking.

The Hartmans?

They're masters of self-promotion. And the spin. With all the research and press coverage I've seen, they close ranks and never—ever—admit fault.

Or apologize.

Somehow, I don't believe Alex will be shaken by seeing his name, along with that of his immediate family, on a suspect list. He's a prosecutor. That alone has taught him how to play a role. To craft a story with precision.

Couple that with the Hartman way, and Alex might be quite the puzzle.

Charlie appears in the doorway. She moves aside and waves Alex in.

He stands there, reminding me of a somewhat shorter version of JJ with his expensive suit.

Alex, however, has more of that highbrow haughtiness that comes from generational wealth, while JJ has more of an easy, confident charm.

"You remember Meg," Charlie says. "And Matt."

Hellos are exchanged along with the obligatory offerings of coffee or other beverage.

Alex refuses all, and Charlie points to the seat beside me, forcing him to walk around the table and come face to face with our murder board.

I make no effort to hide my curiosity as he pauses and takes it all in.

Then he turns, shoulders back, an expression of, well, nothing. Not a worry line. Not a crease. Just that Hartman mask.

Hartmans.

Absolute masters.

He walks to his seat and gestures to the board. "I see the gang is all there. You're missing Eloise."

I roll the name around, but my brain won't latch on. "Eloise?"

"My youngest cousin. She died two years after Tiffany. Leukemia."

Charlie jots the name on her notepad. "Thank you," she says.

"For what it's worth," he says, "the PD cleared her early on, so you may want to spend your time elsewhere."

He may be trying to be helpful, but something about his tone slices against my already fried nerves. As if we're not smart enough to figure it out on our own. As if we need him.

Which we don't.

For kicks, I stand and march to the board, where I add Eloise to the list of names.

Charlie shoots me one of her focused, mean-girl looks. Yes, I'm being a brat. She knows it. I know it.

Everyone in this room knows it.

Ask me if I care.

I reclaim my seat just as Matt leans forward. "What can you tell us about your father?"

I've always adored Matt. No bullshit. No stalling. Just a straight-on inquiry.

Still with the mask of nothingness, Alex meets his eye. "My father. He was a mean bastard who drank too much and took it out on everyone around him."

Alrighty then.

I make a mental note to call my dad and tell him how much I love him.

Charlie flips to a fresh page on her notepad. "Why?"

"My guess," Alex says, "is he didn't want to be carrying the weight of the Hartman legacy."

"We've spoken to Mallory. She indicated there may have been tension between your father and Gerald?"

Alex barks out a laugh. "That's one way to put it. They were cordial, but my uncle was a major part of the problem. When they were younger, my father assumed they'd run the company together. Gerry wound up being a liability on many fronts."

"The party boy," Matt says.

"The party boy who cost us a lot of hush money." Alex waves a hand. "Prostitutes. Drug dealers. Bookies."

"He owed money?" Charlie asks.

"Plenty of it. My father always paid it. But, who knows, there could have been more Gerry didn't tell Dad about."

"Who do you think killed Tiffany?"

This from Charlie. Also no slouch in the directness department.

Alex lets out a low whistle. "No wonder JJ loves you."

My sister averts her gaze, pretending to stare at the murder board. I know her, and underneath that calm facade, she's crumbling.

Clearly, Alex is uninformed about JJ punting their relationship.

"Here's the thing," Alex says, his gaze following Charlie's. "Something happened during that party. My father and Gerry weren't at odds. I was young, but kids understand tension, and it was thick that night." He absently waves a hand. "It's in the reports somewhere."

This is news to me, but I haven't reviewed all the files. Perhaps Mom knows this, but I think she'd have mentioned it.

"I'm not sure," Alex says, "but I've always thought Gerry was in another mess. My father was tired of cleaning up his disasters, and I think Dad may have told him he was done shelling out money."

I swivel my chair to face him. "You're saying Tiffany may have been killed because of Gerry's debts?"

Alex shrugs. "It's not out of the question. Think about it. Why, if Gerry owed some nasty people money, would they kill him? He was their golden goose who would always be back for more action. If he's dead, they definitely don't get their money, and they lose an income stream."

The room falls silent for a moment, and that sickness in my stomach returns.

Yes, there are people who are evil in the world. Those who would murder an innocent child simply to send a message to the degenerate parent.

God, this world is too much for me.

"Gerry went in and out of the party a lot that night," Alex offers. "That seemed to rile Dad up even more."

Matt pulls a face. "Why did Gerry do that?"

"Don't know. Drug deal? To get high? To pay his bookie? There were plenty there who might have fallen into that category."

"Okay." Charlie taps her pen on her notepad. "Maybe Gerry set up a meeting with whoever he owed money to. With so many people on the grounds, it would be easy to slip someone in for a clandestine meeting."

Alex jerks his head. "That's always been my theory."

And, whoa. My spine stiffens. Did he just imply ...

Before I can finish my thought, words tumble from my mouth. "You're saying your cousin was killed because of her father's debts? And it might've been his bookie or your dad who did it?"

11

Charlie

Alex's fingers tap a steady rhythm on the armrest of the chair across from me, the only visible sign he's nervous. His eyes move from Meg's whiteboard to my notepad, then to the modern art canvas on the wall behind me—anywhere but directly at my face.

Patience isn't my strong suit on a good day. Today, I'm anxious, working on an eight-hour sleep deficit, fighting a migraine, and my heart and head have been in a major collision since JJ chose his job over me. *Go Team Charlie.* Every step of this investigation has dug a hole I can't seem to claw my way out of.

I'm not about to cut Alex any slack, though. He's framing and reframing his answer—I see it behind his eyes. He doesn't want to throw a family member under the bus, especially not his father. If I were in his shoes, I'd feel the same way. And while I'm no prosecutor, I've been on the receiving end of a cross-examination enough to know when to strike and when to wait.

Wait, I order myself. *Do not show impatience.*

That doesn't mean I can't try to get under his skin and see who he coughs up as a suspect. I slide some papers aside and find a class photo of Tiffany. Using one of the magnets on the board, I place it in the upper left corner to remind us of why we're here. Who we're doing this for.

Meg catches my eye as I return to my seat, approval flickering across her face.

The gamble pays off. "No way my dad killed her," Alex finally says, his words confident.

"Despite what you've told us about his temper?" I maintain a neutral tone—a skill honed through years of FBI profiling and investigative work.

A shoulder lifts in a half-hearted shrug. "I won't deny that when he'd been at the bottle, he threw things, punched walls, and screamed himself hoarse." He meets my gaze, defiant through a veil of uncertainty. "But murder? Bashing in Tiffany's skull? No way."

Bashing in her skull. I note the distinction he's making—violence against objects versus violence against people. Classic compartmentalization. As a forensic psychologist, I've seen this denial pattern countless times in families of offenders.

"You suggested it could have been an accident," I press, crossing my legs and adjusting my skirt. Today, I've overcompensated for my heartbreak and exhaustion with my favorite Pucci jacquard knit pencil skirt and top. I look fantastic, even if I can barely walk.

"Look, I know how this sounds." Alex rubs the back of his neck, a self-soothing gesture. "Dad was an asshole, but if it had been an accident, he would have admitted to it."

"Alex," I say, purposely using his name to subtly put him on the spot. I shift my expression into what Meg calls my "therapist mask" —attentive but neutral—doodling on my notepad like this is nothing more than a casual conversation. "Speculations aside, what do you think happened to Tiffany?"

His face mirrors mine, his own skill with interrogating criminals giving nothing away. "Doesn't matter what I think, and you know it." His fingers interlace over his stomach, shielding his center. Classic. "You're looking for something to back up what you've already decided."

A flare of irritation hits, but I suppress it. I offer a small, professional smile. "I want your perspective, Alex. No judgments, no preconceptions. This isn't about confirming what I think—it's about understanding what might have happened from someone who knew Tiffany." I point to her picture with my pen.

Alex rubs his hands over the chair arms. "My gut says it wasn't premeditated. What could an eight-year-old have possibly done, seen, or overheard that would upset someone enough to kill her in the midst of a party?"

"Assuming we aren't dealing with a child killer who purposely targeted her," I say.

He doesn't bite. He continues to speculate. "If we take Dad out of the equation, that leaves Gerry. As I mentioned, Gerry had an addiction to pills. He was a playboy. A total screw up." Something about his delivery feels off. Rehearsed. As if he's been turning these alternatives over in his mind for years. Probably has since the case has been reopened at least twice before now. Or maybe Mary fed him those exact lines through the course of his childhood. "Mom always said Gerry would end up dead or in prison. She hated him and that Dad let him hang around."

Hate is a strong word. I casually add another tally mark to my mental Mary Did It column. "But Gerry was there for the entire party?"

"Yeah. The tension between him and Dad was putting a

damper on things, and Mom forced them to take it downstairs. I remember how upset she was. She literally walked the two of them out of the parlor and down the steps."

Of course she did. "To the basement?"

A single nod. Tight. As if he's embarrassed to talk about his uncle's addiction.

"How long were they down there?"

"Fifteen, twenty minutes maybe?"

My mind spins with fresh ideas. Meg and Matt watch me carefully. "Did Tiffany see her father escorted out by your mom?"

"I don't know where she was when it happened."

"So, she might have been in the basement already."

He doesn't agree, but he's following my train of thought.

"Let's assume Gerry was high or asking for money to pay his bookie," I theorize. "He and Phillip were arguing, and things were tense. Mary escorted them downstairs, where Tiffany was already hanging out. Mary was especially outraged that Gerry was ruining her Christmas party, and perhaps things got out of hand. She picked up the nearest heavy object and threw it at him." It's a tough thing to force Alex to imagine, but I want to push him enough to see his reaction. I mimic throwing something. "Tiffany got in the way and ended up dead."

He gapes. A long, horrible pause ensues. Neither Matt nor Meg moves a muscle. "You think my mom killed Tiffany?" He blows a raspberry and rears back in the chair. "That's ridiculous."

His reaction is genuine—absolute shock at the idea. "I'm simply exploring all the ways the scenario could have played out. You took your father off the table. I'm following your reasoning."

His eyes harden. "The Hartmans aren't perfect, my mother included, but we're not monsters."

Someone is.

I start to say exactly that, but JJ's face flashes in my mind—his eyes narrowed in frustration, his frame tense and simmering with anger beneath the surface. *You're obsessed, Charlie. This case is thirty years cold for a reason. Let it go before it costs you everything.*

JJ has never accepted that, for me, some ghosts refuse to rest until justice is served. Maybe that's why we're falling apart—his world is black and white, neat and classified with cases that are either worth pursuing or not. Orders come from the top, and he follows them. My world exists in the gray spaces. In the files that gather dust. In the voices that have been silenced.

I don't take orders from anyone but my conscience.

I force those thoughts away. His theory conveniently shifts blame to either a dead man or the family black sheep. Gerry makes an easy scapegoat. Still, he's alive. Might be worth tracking him down. "An accident explains a lot, but regardless of who did it, why wouldn't they admit to it, if it was an accident?"

"Um, because they killed a child?" Alex's gaze darts to his watch. "Look, I need to get to work. I have a ten o'clock meeting." He shifts in his chair, already mentally out the door. "I hope I was able to shed some light on things."

"One more question." I rise with him. "Any idea what happened to that designer purse I mentioned that Phillip gave Mary that night?"

"Purse?"

"The Sherman. It's not listed in the items recovered from the party."

"I don't remember it. A lot of that night is a blur, to be honest. Mom took all that stuff to the cottage after the police returned it. She said she didn't want to look at it after what had happened to Tiffany."

"Why didn't she donate it to charity?" Meg asks.

A noncommittal shrug. "She said it was all cursed."

At the door, I extend my hand. "If you think of anything else, even something that seems insignificant, please call."

He cups my hand with his. The warmth of his touch surprises me. "Sure, of course. Oh, and I'm sorry about what happened with JJ."

So, he does know. His earlier comment made me think he was in the dark about it.

The way his eyes soften surprises me. The gentleness of his hand. I actually want to like this guy.

I ease out of his grip. "I put him in a bad position. It was to be expected."

Lies, lies, lies. I hate myself for them. I didn't expect it. Not at all. I would have sworn on every tenant I hold sacred that JJ Carrington would never break my heart.

"I put in a request for the footage from the security cameras, by the way," Alex says, back to business. "It's missing. I have an intern looking for it, but my guess is that it has been misplaced somewhere since it was last reviewed five years ago. Sorry."

Another accident. It happens, but what are the odds?

As he pulls away from the building, Meg joins me. The sun is bright, reflecting off the piles of snow. "What do you think?"

"He never should have been allowed to work on this case."

"Is the killer his dad or Mary?"

"I want to believe it's her."

"Me, too."

Our father's car stops at the curb. Mom's imposing figure jumps out of the passenger side. Her raised voice suggests they're arguing, but I can't make out what she's saying. She slams the door and stomps up the sidewalk in the same clothes and boots from yesterday.

"Oh, boy," Meg says.

Mom enters our office like a tornado—a notebook clutched in one hand, her phone in the other, glasses perched precisely on the bridge of her nose. "Was that Alex Hartman?" she demands, not bothering with pleasantries.

This woman is one of the reasons I'm struggling to breathe this morning. "Hello to you, too, Mom." I cross my arms over my chest, a futile shield against her intensity. "Glad you're out of jail, but couldn't you take a few minutes for a shower and change of clothes?"

She waves off my words, stomping down the hall to the meeting room. "What did he say? Is he weaseling into my investigation?"

Her investigation? Meg must see the steam coming out of my ears. She lays a hand on my arm. "I'll bring her up to speed. Why don't you get some fresh coffee?"

But my anger hits the boiling point. I need a target for it. I charge down the hall. "He voluntarily came in and answered our questions." I stand at the head of the conference table, unwilling to give her the satisfaction of falling into our usual dynamic—her interrogating, me answering. "We have several new leads to follow, thanks to him. *Him*, Mother, not you."

Mom's mouth thins. "Sometimes you need to shake the tree to see what falls out."

What the hell does that mean? Is that an excuse for what she's done? "And sometimes you need to respect boundaries." Meg and Matt sit stock still in their seats, both avoiding looking at either of us. "Your reckless behavior has cost me..." I pause, pulling back before I say something unforgivable. "Has cost *us* too much. If you want our help, back the hell off and let Meg, Matt, and me do our job."

A hush falls. Time stretches out, charged with decades of similar standoffs. I can almost hear the unspoken reminders of all the times she put us first—of the journalism career she shelved for our sake.

"What did Alex say?" She emphasizes each word. Impatience radiates from her. "Did he give you anything useful? Anything I can follow up on?"

Part of me wants to shut her out completely—punishment for my ruined relationship. But the rational side of my brain knows her instincts might spot something we've missed.

And JJ's decision to break up with me isn't her fault. I'm projecting.

The truth that no one is to blame but me nearly crushes me.

"Charlie." Mom's eyes lock onto mine with the same penetrating stare that makes corrupt politicians and evasive police chiefs squirm. "This isn't about me or my tactics right now. This is about finding the truth."

I exhale slowly, regaining what composure I can. She's right. We have competing theories and need to get focused. Tiffany was an innocent child, and nothing in my experience leads me to think this was a personal vendetta. No. It was unplanned. Accidental.

The chair squeals against the floor as I pull it out and sit. "Alex thinks his father might have been involved, but he's conflicted about it. Phillip was a 'mean drunk,'—his words—and his uncle Gerry, Tiffany's father, was into illegal narcotics and gambling." I give her the juicy bits to bring her up to speed, then finish with, "Alex stated there was a family feud that night, and we suspect it escalated over a drug buy or money issue. Gerry could have even had his bookie at the party and wanted Phillip to pay him off. Tiffany may have been accidentally killed trying to defend her dad from the bookie, drug dealer, Phillip, or even Mary. We're not ruling out any of them as our killer."

Mom frowns. "Accidentally killed? That's absurd. Complete nonsense."

"Why do you say that?"

She flips open her weathered notebook. "The autopsy report clearly states that Tiffany's death was not accidental. The blow to her head was delivered with significant force, not consistent with someone stumbling into a fight."

Meg shuffles through papers with purpose. She holds up one of them. "Mom's right, the ME's report states the injury was made deliberately and came from behind. The imprint matched the size and shape of a hammer but not any of the three found on the property. The ME refused to make a definitive call on what the murder weapon was." She mimics someone swinging the tool. "If I were aiming at another adult, I might clip an average eight-year-old in the temple or graze the top of her head. To hit her at the base of her skull, I would have to swing upward, almost like golfing."

Bashing in her skull. The words echo in my head. "Medical examiners can make mistakes." I hate to throw shade at them, but I've been involved in a few cases where it's happened. "Not often, but if Tiffany was shoved backward, she might have tripped and hit her head on a piece of furniture or something."

Mom scribbles notes in such a demented scrawl, I'm surprised she can even read them. "Sounds like there were plenty of issues for Phillip and Gerry to fight about, and Mary escorting them to the basement implicates her. Why didn't Alex tell the police this?"

The migraine looms larger. "He was nine, Mom."

"I mean, once he was grown?"

"That he didn't take all this to the police suggests he's scared one of his parents did the deed. We need to look into all of these angles."

"Good job with the interrogation and getting his story to fall apart under scrutiny."

Her compliment makes Meg smile. I just rub my temple. "The lingering question is whether that's because he was young and his memory is faulty, or because he's covering for someone."

"Mary," Meg and Mom say at the same time.

Where Mom bursts through doors, Matt carefully picks the locks. He taps a thumb on the table, brow furrowed. "We should also consider the possibility of a departmental cover-up. This is D.C. and an influential family—we've all seen it happen."

"True." Mom scribbles some more. She loves a good conspiracy theory involving law enforcement.

I stare at the whiteboard. "Criminal psychology 101: People rarely tell complete lies when a partial truth will do. They mix fact with fiction. Real emotions with misdirection. Alex could be protecting his mom or dad by emphasizing certain aspects of the story while downplaying others. Phillip can't defend himself anymore." I pause. "And Alex isn't technically blaming him. He's defending the man, while also planting the idea that he's guilty."

Matt nods, sorting through possibilities. "But his belief in his father's innocence could be genuine, even if misplaced."

Meg jumps up and goes to the board, grabbing a marker. "I don't buy it. He's using his father as a scapegoat, but it's got to be Mary. Think about it. She had means and opportunity."

"No motive," Matt says, "Unless it was an accident, and there were dozens of others in the house that night that also had means and opportunity."

"No motive that *we know of*," I correct. "What if it has to do with that dumb purse? Tiffany played with it, spilled a drink on it, tore it, or somehow damaged it. Mary got mad and lashed out."

Mom snorts. "That's a stretch. Killing the girl over something so trivial?"

"That bag was worth a lot, even back then," Meg says. "A rare designer bag, given to her from her husband as a Christmas gift to make up for some of his slights. Maybe Mary was drunk, saw the damage, and shoved Tiffany. She fell and whacked her head."

"Or Mary smacked her on the back of the head when Tiffany was running away." It's an ugly scenario but possible. "She didn't mean to kill her, yet managed to hit her hard enough that she did."

We sit in silence, the only sound my mother's pen scratching across a page. "Alex didn't answer my question when I asked what he thinks happened," I muse. "Instead, he told us what he wants us to think might have happened."

Meg taps the whiteboard. "I say we narrow our focus to Mary."

Blinders are never good in any investigation. "We can't rule out Phillip and Gerry. To cover all of our bases, we need to consider Mallory, too. If Gerry was a playboy and a drug addict, maybe she'd had enough and confronted him that night. Tiffany jumped between her arguing parents and ended up dead. They covered it up."

Meg circles the four names. "What's next?"

"I've got to interview Mary," Mom says.

"That's not going to happen." I sip my cold coffee. She glares at me. I glare back. "Gerry is our next play. We track him down and get him to talk about his family. See if he points a finger at Phillip or Mary. Or even his ex-wife."

"We need to find the murder weapon," Matt says.

That would be asking for a miracle. "If the police didn't, I doubt we can."

"You're assuming whoever killed Tiffany wanted to get rid of the hammer, so they disposed of it," Mom interjects.

"Wouldn't you? They probably tossed it in the Potomac." I go to the board and tap on HAMMER anyway. "First, we talk to Gerry and get his take on Phillip, Mary, and Mallory. Then, we establish if Mary's purse had anything to do with it. If Gerry provides us with a lead or we acquire new information about that bag, we might have enough evidence for JJ to obtain a search warrant. Then we can look for the missing murder weapon."

"Okay," Mom says. "What do you want me to focus on?"

For a heartbeat, I'm stunned. She's letting me take the lead? I blink, do a silent internal cheer, and regroup yet again. "You and Meg hunt down some of these other folks in the family and get them to collaborate or contradict Alex's statements about Phillip and Gerry." I point at myself. "I'll talk to Janelle about revisiting the forensic evidence. She wasn't the ME back then, but a second opinion on the wound might confirm if we're on the right track about the hammer." I then point to Matt. "You work your contacts at City Hall. Get property records for the Hartman estate, including anything on that safe room installation, tunnel, cottage, everything. We also need to know if the Hartmans owned, or still own, any storage units or secondary properties. Oh, and if you can figure out a way to talk to Mary's daughter, Christina, about the bag without tipping our hand, do it. I feel like she might be a gold mine of intel on that family."

"On it," Matt says, getting up.

Haley walks in and hands me a courier envelope. "This just came for you."

I rip open the tab at the top, and a USB falls out.

"What is it?" Meg asks.

A single piece of paper is stuck inside the cardboard. I snag it, and my knees nearly buckle at the familiar handwriting. "A gift." The corners of my mouth tug up. I show them the USB. "This is the missing security footage from that night."

"From Alex?" Meg asks. "Guess his intern found it."

"Not Alex." My smile breaks free. "Someone else in the AG's office who might still believe in our mission, regardless of what he said yesterday."

Her eyes widen. "JJ?"

I clutch the thumb drive. The pounding in my head fades as my pulse races. "JJ," I confirm. "Let's have a look."

12

Meg

Charged energy fills the room while Charlie downloads the thumb drive to her laptop.

Despite JJ sending this footage, he's on my shit list. I understand his passion for the job, but really? Dumping my sister?

If I didn't think Charlie would bury me alive, I'd call him myself and blast him.

I may risk it anyway.

"Meg!"

Charlie's sharp tone snaps me from my spiraling thoughts, and I swivel to face her. The artist in me can't help but notice the flush in her cheeks. The spark in her eyes is classic Charlie. If we weren't deep into a murder case, I'd be sketching her.

We Schocks get off on our work.

Even when our souls are crushed.

Charlie passes me the thumb drive. "Download everything

to your laptop. Then back it up to the cloud. We're not taking any chances."

Since I don't have it with me, I set the drive on the table while Charlie hammers away at her keyboard.

"I'll put it on the big screen," she says.

Seconds later—voila—a grainy, black and white video appears on the large television mounted on the wall.

I once hated that thing. I thought it was tacky.

Now?

Not so tacky.

Mom slides into the chair next to Matt, the two of them swiveling to face the television.

"This is good," she says. "We can study it frame by frame."

"Great," Matt deadpans, his voice flat. "I'll clear my day."

Indeed.

Charlie taps her keyboard, and footage rolls of what appears to be the front of the Hartman mansion.

"That's the front," Mom says.

"And?" I ask, heavy on the sarcasm since we're not blind and can see that.

"Well," Mom claps back, upping the ante on the sarcasm. "If you were meeting with your drug dealer or bookie, would you do it in front for everyone to see or somewhere out back? The main grounds and cottage are behind the house. If you wanted to sneak around and do deals or get high, you'd do it there. You'd leave through the kitchen door. At the rear of the house."

Gotta give it to Mom on that one.

"I'll buy that," I say, pointing at the laptop. "Charlie, do you have footage from the yard?"

She moves her finger over the mousepad and juts her chin at the television, where a menu with different tiles appears.

"There." Matt points at the screen. "Lower left says kitchen door."

A click from Charlie yields another grayscale image, the

quality so poor I squint and crane my neck closer as if that'll help me see better. Security footage has come a long way in thirty years.

"For people with so much money," Mom says, "you'd think they'd have invested in a better system. With sound."

Charlie grunts and shoots me her I-may-have-to-kill-our-mother look.

I offer her a sympathetic smile and turn my attention back to Mom. "Check your notes. What time was the murder?"

"I don't have to. The estimated time of death was nine-thirty."

Using her mouse, Charlie drags the button below the video to the right and clicks.

"Eight o'clock," I say. "Keep going."

She tries twice more before she lands on nine-fifteen, clicks the play button, and sits back.

The video shows a group of kids of various ages hanging out in the yard. Three younger kids lie in the snow, making angels, while what appear to be older teenagers stand around watching.

As irritated as I am with Mom, I have to agree with her on the sound issue. It would be nice to have color images, as well as the option to hear what's being said.

"Charlie," I say, "can you zoom in on the younger kids? Maybe Tiffany is one of them."

She does, but the already hazy video blurs even more.

"Two boys and a girl," Charlie says.

"Tiffany had blonde hair," Matt adds.

I focus on the girl in the image, swinging her arms and legs and smiling over her snow angel efforts. She's not wearing a hat, and lying on the ground as she is, her hair blends with the snow.

"Even in grayscale," I say, "light versus dark stands out. Her hair is light."

"Meg's right," Mom says. "I don't think that's her, though. Tiffany's face was rounder."

"Mom," Charlie says, "who are those boys on the ground? Do you recognize them?"

She shakes her head. "No. But I have a list in my notes of everyone in attendance."

"Do they look like Alex?"

Mom stands and moves closer to the screen, studying it for a moment before shaking her head. "I don't think either of them is Alex. They look too young. And the ones standing are too old."

Interesting. "So, Alex and Tiffany aren't in this shot?"

"Doesn't appear so."

I push out of my chair, move to the murder board, and grab a marker. At the bottom of my myriad of notes, I draw a line, put a hash mark in the middle, and label it nine-thirty.

"The estimated time of death," I say, "is nine-thirty, and we're looking at video shot at nine-fifteen. We have no idea where Tiffany was at this time, and I'm wondering why she's not with these kids who are close to her age. If time of death is accurate, I don't think it's a stretch to think the murder could be happening while these kids are playing in the snow."

Matt clucks his tongue. "Time of death could easily be off by fifteen minutes. Hell, she could already be dead at this point."

I twirl my marker at Charlie. "Get to nine-thirty. See if there's anything suspicious?"

Charlie does her thing, dragging the icon a bit to the right and ... nothing.

The screen goes black.

"Whoa," I say, turning to Charlie. "What happened?"

She holds her hands palms up and lets out a huff. "No idea."

Matt swivels to face her. "Did you accidentally exit or something?"

"I didn't touch it."

"Dirty bastards," Mom says. "Someone erased the footage."

Mom. Always the conspiracy theorist.

"For once," Charlie hammers away at the keyboard. "I don't think you're nuts. I'm sending this to Teeg."

Teeg. What he can do with a computer never fails to amaze.

Matt nods. "He might be able to tell if it's been tampered with." He spins back to the television. "Once you're done sending it, let's watch that last few minutes again."

Two minutes later, Charlie resets the video, hits play, and we watch a bunch of kids loitering around the back door of the mansion. No Gerry or other adults, though.

"Wait!" Mom stabs her finger at the screen. "Zoom out, Charlie! There. On the right. See that?"

My mother makes me insane. She really does. But when I see her like this? All lit up and excited?

I get where Charlie and I come from. Where our obsessive desire for justice was born.

Charlie does as instructed, and a person—well, part of a person—comes into view. The camera angle isn't wide enough, only allowing for a profile.

I study the image, capturing details. Oversized coat, ugly hat, collar turned up.

No hair is visible, so if it's a woman, her hair is either very short or tucked into the hat.

The person is taller than the teens, but from this angle, it's impossible to determine gender.

"Damn," I say, "Can you zoom out more? Give me a better look?"

"No. That's it. The camera must have been fixed, so we can't see all of whoever that is."

She rewinds to right before the person comes into view,

stepping out the back door, and staying to the periphery of where the kids are.

On purpose?

If they'd just committed a murder, maybe.

"Look how he's hunched over," Mom says. "As if trying to hide something under that giant coat."

Okay. Now she's getting crazy. "You're assuming," I say, "it's a man. Let's not get ahead of ourselves on the hiding something. There's no way to tell that. It was cold. They could be trying to stay warm."

She pins me with a heated look that takes me back to my childhood when I decided I wanted a mural and took a marker to my freshly painted bedroom wall.

"Or hiding a murder weapon," Mom says.

"Whoever that is," Matt says, "knew where the blind spots were."

Mom smacks her hand against the credenza. "Yes! That's our killer! I'm sure of it!"

"Relax, Mom," Charlie says. "Let's think about this."

Matt peers at us and cocks his head. "Someone who lives—or works—at the house might know the camera locations."

Charlie angles her chair toward my murder board. "Meg, let's list all the people who lived or worked at the house who might know the security system."

With Mom's help, we identify six. Mary and her husband. Alex and his sister, Christina. The full-time housekeeper and nanny.

"Those are only the ones who have regular access to the house," Matt says. "There could be landscapers or maintenance people. Whoever installed and/or monitors the system would know. Plus, there are the guards at the gate."

The guards. During our previous meeting at the U.S. Attorney's office, Alex had said that his family had been receiving threats due to financial issues and layoffs.

"I forgot about them," I say. "The Hartmans had a rotation that operated the gate."

"Were they there 24/7?" Matt asks.

"For the most part," Mom says. "From what I saw, it was rare that there wasn't someone there. And they always had someone at the gate during events."

"They would all know," Charlie says, "from viewing the footage, what the camera angles were."

I tap my timeline. "Playing devil's advocate here. Let's assume this person is the murderer and they're leaving the house at nine-twentyish, that means the murder happened before nine-thirty."

"The nine-one-one call." Mom marches to the corner where we've stacked her research boxes. "I have a transcript somewhere. Everyone, take a box."

Then we're all in motion, and Matt hefts them onto the table, each of us taking one.

I lift a lid and groan at the number of files. We might be here a while. "Mom, do you remember who placed the initial call?"

"Of course. It was Mary."

13

———

Charlie

Gordy Jarrett's hands tremble as he pours coffee into three mismatched mugs. The clink of ceramic against ceramic echoes through his modest living room, where faded security certification plaques compete with fishing trophies for wall space. I called Gerald but got his voicemail. I debated leaving a message or trying again later, but even though the case is thirty years old, I feel like I'm on the clock. Time is slipping away. I left a brief voicemail, asking him to get in touch.

My skirt pinches at my thighs as I perch on the edge of the worn leather sofa, and the designer heels feel wildly out of place for this part of town.

"Fired, not retired," he says, handing me a mug with a fishing quote that reads, *The best way to catch a fish is to let him think he's escaping.* Huh. Same for criminals. "I was with the Hartmans for sixteen years, and one dead kid later, I'm bagging groceries part-time." He settles his substantial frame into a recliner that creaks in protest. "Didn't get back into security until I took a guard job at a bank."

I've interviewed enough suspects to know when someone is constructing a narrative that casts themselves as the victim. It's a classic deflection technique, but that doesn't mean he's guilty of anything beyond self-pity. "Why did they fire you?"

"I was head of security. My job was to keep the family safe." He picks at a snag on the arm's upholstery. "I failed, but God's truth, I never thought that girl was in danger."

"Mr. Jarrett—"

"Gordy, please. Mr. Jarrett was my father, God rest him."

"Gordy," I continue, trying not to make a face at the bitterness of the coffee. "Who do you think killed her?"

"Not a clue, sweetheart," he says. "Could have been anybody."

If he had worked for the family for that long, surely he must've suspected someone. I switch tactics. "We're trying to understand what happened the night Tiffany died. Not just the facts listed in the police report but the dynamics, the personalities involved."

"I saw you on the TV with your mom." He makes a whirling motion around his temple with a finger. "She's a crazy ol' gal, ain't she?"

She's been called worse. Doesn't mean his comment doesn't annoy me. I sip the bitter coffee in order to hold my tongue.

Mom would be here if it weren't for the fact that the current number one journalist on YouTube called our office asking for an interview. I don't know whether to be relieved or horrified that she picked that over Gordy.

Meg chuckles and lays her classic warm, inviting smile on him. "What was Tiffany like?"

His eyes fix on the distance beyond my shoulder. "Don't like speaking ill of the dead. 'Specially kids. Don't seem right."

My gut tightens. That type of disclaimer usually preceded something damning.

"We feel the same way." Meg gives a sympathetic nod and lowers her voice. "But the truth can't hurt her now."

God, she's good.

Gordy fidgets with his pant leg, brushing away an invisible speck of lint. Or maybe the emotions he's feeling. "Truth is, she was a bit of a snot. Smart as a whip but mean with it. You know the type? The ones who figure out which buttons to push. That family is full of them."

Like Phillip, the mean drunk. I nod, keeping my face neutral. "Did you notice anything unusual about her behavior that night? Any notable interactions with the guests?"

He barks a humorless laugh. "Besides taking Alex's cherished hockey stick and hiding it in the panic room? That was pretty notable."

Meg locks eyes with me. My pulse spikes. "Tell us about that."

"Signed by Wayne Gretzky. Gift from his dad. Phillip traveled all the time and brought back outlandish gifts to Alex and Christina to ease his guilt." Gordy shakes his head. "Tiff waited until everyone was occupied with the party and swiped it from its prized spot in his room. Then told him she'd hidden it in the new panic room."

Why would he need Gordy to fetch it? "He couldn't find it?"

"The room wasn't finished." Gordy sets his mug down on the side table with a thunk. "State-of-the-art for 1995, but the security panel only worked from the outside at that point. Contractor was coming back after the holidays to finish the interior controls."

"And?" Meg asks.

Gordy spreads his hands like his point is obvious. "If Alex went in, she could lock him inside."

A safe room turned trap. "Alex was afraid to go after it."

Gordy's eyes darken. "Wouldn't have been the first time she pulled a stunt like that. She locked the gardener's kid in the pool house for three hours that August. Boy nearly got heatstroke."

Meg's face falls. "That's awful."

I remember similar childhood stunts between us, the Wonder Twins. The time she pushed me out of the oak tree in the woods because I broke her favorite paintbrush. Or when I shoved her into a boulder for putting a spider in my hair. She ended up with a knot on her head; I got two months of laundry duty and a deep-seated fear of bugs.

Kid-on-kid bullying isn't abnormal. "What happened with the hockey stick?"

"Alex came to me all upset. Asked if I'd get it when I was doing my rounds." Gordy's expression softens. "Good kid. Didn't want to tattle to his parents and make a scene at their fancy party. Just wanted his stick back."

Meg sips her coffee. How does she drink that without gagging? "And you got it for him?"

"Course I did. Part of the job—protecting what matters to the people you're paid to look after. I'd done the same for Christina and some of the other kids when they needed something and their parents were too busy or too drunk." His face takes on a wistful pride. "Found the thing propped in the corner and brought it to the boy's room without anyone being the wiser."

The panic room. Orbiting the crime, but never quite touching it. "Did you tell the police?" We know he didn't, or at least I assume so. If Matt's theory about dirty cops is true, maybe it was expunged.

Gordy stiffens. "Wasn't asked about it. They wanted to know about security protocols and who had access to which areas inside the house. Not kid drama."

"You didn't think it was relevant that Tiffany had demonstrated knowledge of—and interest in—the room near the spot where she later died?"

His face reddens. "At the time, no. It just seemed like one more mean trick from that girl. Not a..." He trails off, swallowing hard.

Thirty years, and it still troubles him. That says something. I believe him, despite myself. Sometimes the most damning evidence against someone is their conscience.

Meg catches my eye, her fingers tapping against her ripped jeans—a silent signal that I need to tread gently or lose our best lead at the moment.

"Mr. Jarrett. Gordy," I say gently, "did you see Gerald or Phillip arguing that night?"

His face clears. "Those two? They were always in each other's faces. Upstairs, downstairs, probably argued in both that night. A lot of society drama, you know. Always was. Gads, I hated those parties."

"But you didn't directly witness any argument between them in the basement?"

"Nope."

"Or between Mary and Gerry?" Meg adds.

"Mary didn't speak to that scumbag unless she had to. Ever. Why?"

Meg squeezes her cup. "You're sure?"

"A hundred percent, sweetheart. Gerry went on the patio to smoke a cigarette off and on, but so did half the other guests. Mary snuck out to the cottage."

I freeze. "Mary left the house?"

"Sure did."

"You saw her?"

"On that night's surveillance tape."

Meg and I exchange a glance. Gordy thinks we don't believe him. He pushes to his feet, knees popping. "I can prove it. Before they canned me, I took the backup of that night's tape. Still got it."

"You have a copy of the surveillance footage?"

"Insurance." A bitter smile plays on his lips. "Rich folks always need a fall guy. I worked security long enough to know to cover my ass. Wasn't sure what I might need that video for, but better safe than sorry. You get me?"

Meg frowns and shoots me a questioning look. "Is that...?"

"Legal?" Gordy finishes. "Not according to my employment contract. But wrongful termination ain't nice, either. I had two kids in school. Sometimes you need leverage."

Family first. Our dad would have done the same. "Is there anything suspicious on the tape? Anything at all?"

A shake of his head. "Watched it dozens of times. I do feel somewhat responsible, you know? It was my job to keep everyone safe in that house." His eyes cloud. "That girl died on my watch. I wondered if I'd missed something."

How many times have I replayed interviews in my head, wondering if I missed a verbal tell, a micro-expression that might have changed an investigation's outcome? "Did you? Miss something?"

"Nah. Never saw anything that looked like foul play."

"But you still have the copy?"

Gordy jerks his thumb at another room. "In the basement. I'll get it."

Meg rises and sets her mug on the coffee table. As a forensic sculptor, she deals primarily with physical evidence—bones, tissue markers, facial reconstructions. But she understands, as I do, what this could mean. Video evidence from a security system could reveal truths that memories—faded, biased, or deliberately tampered with—can't. "You think it'll show something more than we have?" she whispers. "He could be the one who erased the footage."

"Maybe," I admit. "But if his copy hasn't been tampered with, we can either cross a few people off our suspect list or narrow that list down."

Thumps and muttering come from below. Gordy returns, dust streaking his shirt and a black plastic case in his hand. "State of the art back then," he tells us, blowing dust off an old VHS tape. "Sixteen cameras throughout the property, all time-stamped, backed up every twelve hours." His wrinkled fingers tap the cassette. "One tape held twenty-four hours of footage. This is the backup copy from that night."

He shuffles to an entertainment center that looks like it was purchased during the Clinton Administration and slides the tape into a VCR—an actual functioning VCR. He turns on a much newer flat screen and fiddles with the VCR. "For that time, it was impressive. Motion-activated in some zones, constant recording in others. Split-screen view of all cameras, but you could isolate any feed." The screen flickers to blue, then displays a grainy multi-camera view of the Hartman estate. "Still, I did a manual backup as routine. You never know when technology is going belly up, you know?"

My eyes gobble up the layout—entrances, exits, blind spots. This is much more intricate than the copy we have. "Can you advance to around nine-twenty?"

He fast-forwards, causing the machine to whir. The time-stamp in the corner blurs as figures move at comical speeds. Guests arriving at the party, kids go out back to have a snowball fight, while some make angels. "Here we go." He slows as the counter approaches 21:19:42.

The screen shows multiple angles of the mansion. "There." I point as a figure emerges. "Can you isolate that feed?"

"Afraid not," he says. "State of the art thirty years ago, but it ain't digital."

The person we couldn't fully make out with our version steps out into the snow. This is where the other footage turned to static.

His doesn't. "You're sure that isn't Gerry?" I squint at the grainy footage. At least it's on a big screen. The figure moves with purpose through the accumulated snow, heading directly toward the cottage.

Gordy shakes his head. "That's Mary. That god-awful hat." He laughs. "Ugliest thing I ever saw with those weird pom-poms. She claimed it was some fancy designer and wore it all winter that year."

One more nail in that woman's coffin.

On screen, she reaches the cottage door, glances back toward the main house, and quickly slides something from beneath her coat.

"What is that?" Meg asks, also moving to get closer to the pixelated image.

"Not sure," Gordy says. "One of her purses, I think."

She enters, leaving the door open, and appears a few seconds later without the item in hand, locking the door behind her as she leaves. Head down, she hurries to the kitchen door, her footprints the only evidence of her journey through the pristine snow.

"The Sherman bag," Meg whispers. "She took it to the cottage."

The nudge in my brain is full-on screaming. "She did this before she called nine-one-one." I face Gordy. "Didn't you suspect Mary could have been hiding evidence that night? That purse could have contained the murder weapon."

His weathered face registers genuine shock. He leans back in his chair, the springs creaking. "Evidence? No, no. Mary always snuck out there to smoke. Phillip hated her addiction, said it wasn't ladylike, but she'd been doing it for years."

"You're saying this was routine?"

"Her nerves were shot because of the party." He sounds like he has a crush on her. "Phillip drank, Mary smoked. All those rich folks under one roof? She was leaving a fresh carton of cigarettes out there. She pretends—pretended—to love parties, but she didn't. I figured she was stashing a fresh supply for later. She'd slip out for a cigarette break when nobody was looking. Phillip would've thrown a fit if he caught her smoking during one of his fancy gatherings."

Mary tampered with the security tape. Over her smoking? Hard to believe that. "But you saw her hiding something specific on this occasion, and you didn't report it."

"The cops had the same video I do. She had me take a copy of it to them the next morning. If they didn't question her about it, why would I? I didn't think anything of it."

The hair on the back of my neck tingles. "The *next morning*? Why didn't they confiscate the tape that night?"

He splays his fingers. "There was no intruder. Everyone there had been invited. She said all the cops wanted to confirm was the comings and goings of the guests."

Meg raises a brow at me. "Is that normal? To wait that long afterward to get their hands on the tape?"

"Depends on the detective in charge, but Gordy's right. The footage is only of the outside grounds. The girl was killed inside, and probably by one of the guests or family." And this gave Mary plenty of time to alter the original tape. She just didn't know that Gordy was actually a pretty damn good guard who made routine backups of them because he didn't trust the technology. "They wouldn't automatically prioritize exterior footage that night unless they suspected an intruder, which they didn't."

"Family?" Gordy's voice turns shocked again. "You honestly think someone in the family killed Tiff?"

This isn't the time to admit that I sure as hell do, at least not to this near stranger. He doesn't know that the original footage has been tampered with. "Did Mary know how to run the security recording software?"

Gordy rubs his jaw. "Sort of. She sometimes watched the recorded footage, and then told me when to erase the tapes so we could reuse them. She kept a few, like ones that showed some of her more famous friends coming to the house." He lets go of a giant sigh and shakes his head. "Look, I'll be the first to admit Mary's no angel. She's assertive and bossy, and her ego is bigger than my whole house. Some might even say Tiffany learned a lot from her, but she'd never kill a little girl. Never. Why would she?"

I consider his question. Because Tiffany taunted her son? Scared him? It does seem like overkill, but it doesn't exonerate her. Why else would she erase that footage? "Motive can be complex, layered, and sometimes invisible even to the perpetrators themselves. Mary might have had reasons you didn't see."

Meg gets the same look when she's about to bring a face back from obscurity. "We need a copy of this tape."

"Ain't gonna get me in trouble, is it?" Gordy asks.

I can't guarantee that. I also can't let this disappear back into his basement. "Your help could bring a killer to justice," I tell him. It's a too-often-used statement these days, but still effective.

I hope.

He frowns, unconvinced.

My sister works her magic. "This is circumstantial, and nothing will probably come from it, but we do need to review it with our team. You don't owe the Hartmans anything, remember? They fired you over this, and it wasn't your fault."

He doesn't move. Doesn't say anything. I try another tactic. "You made a copy and kept this tape. You're in a legal gray area."

From his body language, I'm pretty sure he's not our killer, and if he is? He's a better actor than Mary. I see him wavering.

"We'll pay you." I dig in my purse and pull out the last of my cash. "A hundred dollars."

Gordy's eyes get the glint of someone who's reconsidering his loyalties. Since Meg has hit on one of his emotional triggers, he can justify giving us the copy and making a buck at the same time. "Let me see what I can do."

Meg gives me a high-five behind his back.

Less than ten minutes later, we walk out with a copy of the true original. It's on another blasted VCR tape, but Matt should be able to convert it to a digital file without too much trouble.

"Could the hockey stick be the murder weapon?" I ask Meg.

She shakes her head. "Even if the killer used the end, it wouldn't have cracked her skull like that."

"Couldn't hide that in a purse, either," I mutter as I merge onto the freeway.

"Are we taking this to JJ?"

"Eventually," I say.

"Mom is going to love you forever. This could crack the case open."

"Mom is going to have to give me a loan. And before we show it to her, we're going to confront Mary."

Meg whips her head to look at me. "You can't be serious. She'll have us thrown in jail."

I grin. "Not if I break her first."

"You're not waiting to hear back from Gerald?"

"Nope. I've got a feeling he's going to give us nothing but excuses, and after what we saw on this tape, we know Mary is the one who left the house and hid something in the cottage."

"What are you planning?"

"To bluff my ass off and get a confession. You up for playing bad cop/good cop?"

"Only if I get to be the badass."

We both know that's not her style. I pat her arm. "Let's play it by ear."

14

Meg

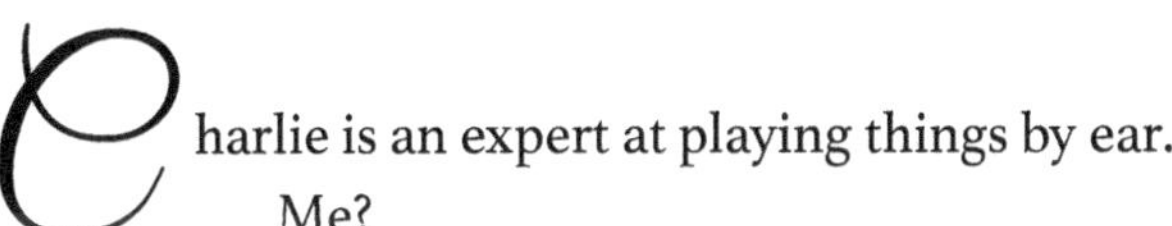

Charlie is an expert at playing things by ear.

Me?

I like a certain sense of order and having a plan. Some might call me methodical. I'm not sure I'd go that far, but there's peace in knowing what comes next.

It's part of why I love forensic sculpting. I start with a skull and, using charts and data that provide me with measurements for anatomic points, I begin to rebuild a face. I cut tissue depth markers, glue them to the skull, place prosthetic eyes into the sockets, and slowly layer clay over the markers.

Layer by layer, the person comes to life.

Talk about methodical.

It's a process that takes hours upon hours, but there's something about watching it develop that enthralls me.

As much as I love having a plan, sometimes Charlie's way is better.

This time, I hope we're not the ones in a jail cell.

As if on cue, Charlie's phone rings and Mom's name lights up the dashboard screen.

She's probably tired of waiting for an update.

"Here we go," Charlie mutters and taps the steering wheel. "Hi, Mom."

"Where are you?"

Mom's voice comes fast and breathy, putting me on edge. I know this voice. It's the one that means something is happening, and it's not necessarily good.

Charlie glances at me, then focuses back on the freeway. The blur of cars flying by like we're standing still.

Adrenaline fires my system, so I do what I always do when Mom goes a little nuts. I draw a slow breath, lift my chin, and shove my shoulders back while I wait for whatever news she's about to level us with.

"What happened?" I ask.

"You need to get back here."

I close my eyes, force myself to stay patient with our drama queen mother, who hasn't answered my question. "Mom, what's wrong?"

"Well," she says, "obviously, you're not listening to the news."

At this, my sister offers a grunt—one that usually leads to a smart-ass retort. Not today. I don't have the energy for another round of their banter.

Between the Gordy meeting, the puzzle-piecing, and the general brain drain, I'm running on fumes. I need food and ten blessed minutes of silence.

Except...Mom.

"We just got out of our meeting," I say, reaching for my phone to check the news.

A text from Jerome flashes across the screen.

Guilt hits me like a sledgehammer. I've been avoiding him

—using the case as an excuse—but Jerome isn't stupid. He knows I've been dodging him since he brought up marriage.

"Hello?" Mom asks.

I swipe the text away. "Hold on. I'm pulling up the local news."

"Charlie," Mom says, her voice direct, "you're not going to be happy. And I'm sorry."

Once again, my sister shoots me a look and then shifts her attention back to driving. "What did you do?"

"Ha!" Mom barks. "My eldest daughter. You're a tough cookie. This time it wasn't me. We've got a horde of press outside the office. Both front and back."

We haven't been gone that long. What in the hell could have happened?

Welcome to the world of Schock.

My question is answered as soon as I tap on my news app, and the lead headline populates the screen.

Former FBI Profiler Accused of Misconduct. My stomach twists into a painful knot. Charlie is a former FBI profiler, and it doesn't take a rocket scientist to understand this is what has Mom spun up. I tap into the article.

Charlize Schock. Former FBI profiler. Local investigator renowned for solving cold cases.

Head pounding, I skip ahead, scanning for the meat of it. *Improper sexual relationship with FBI supervisor.*

What? My jaw drops.

Charlie? Sleeping with her boss?

That's ridiculous.

JJ's name appears next, and suddenly, this smear job is more personal.

And public.

Other than the names being right, the article contains no facts or evidence, only an 'anonymous tip.'

"Shit," I whisper.

What else is there to say when they've paired a lie with a fact because Charlie is involved with JJ.

"Meg," Charlie says, "what is it?"

I set my phone in my lap and shift to face my sister. "Take the next exit. We need to pull over and make a plan. Now."

Without a word, she changes lanes and exits.

"A plan for what?"

I point to a gas station at the bottom of the ramp. "Pull in there. Mom, we'll call you back."

She hangs up without arguing, and Charlie zips into the gas station and parks off to the side.

"What the hell, Meg?"

I hand her the phone. "There's no easy way to say this. An article just dropped. It accuses you of sleeping with your FBI boss to get plum cases. JJ's name is mentioned, suggesting you were also using sex to manipulate him."

A few beats of silence pass while she processes. It's as if we're suspended in time. Floating between reality and fiction while Charlie absorbs my words.

My sister? Some have called her the original ice queen. Her skin is so thick you could make tires with it. Dump truck tires. Control is her game, and she will never, ever, let anyone see her sweat.

But I know her. Probably better than anyone. I'm an artist, I study people and mannerisms and emotions.

I know her.

Underneath the tough exterior, she's coming apart inch by painful inch.

It's what makes her so good. She's an extraordinary blend of grit and empathy. It's part of why we do what we do with these cold cases, because this stuff?

It's not easy.

Soul-crushing stuff that we dive headfirst into time and time again.

Charlie scrolls. Her cheeks lose all color. Her shoulders sink.

I want to scream. Someone did this to her. Made her feel small. Mary Hartman. Has to be. Who else would go that low?

"Charlie?"

For a few seconds, she squeezes her eyes closed, and I stay quiet, giving her space to gather herself.

Then I see it—the shift. The quiet reclaiming of power.

"Mary," I say. "It has to be her. It's all lies."

"Damn straight."

"What do you want to do?"

"I have to make a statement. I need to talk to JJ and—damn it. Garrett."

Her former FBI boss.

"He'll lose his mind," she continues. "If he's not already. His reputation is everything to him. This stunt is a beauty." She huffs. "But it's not going to scare me off. This only proves the Hartmans have something to hide. I cannot wait to talk Mary."

"We should huddle up back at the office. You can give the press there a statement, we'll triage and then visit Mary."

Charlie nods. "Agreed." She shifts the car into drive. "We've got the next fifteen minutes to come up with a good sound bite."

Twenty minutes later, we shove through the back door of the office, breathless and rattled after being swarmed by the local press. This is what celebrities feel like—trapped by cameras, stalked by paparazzi.

Before we were even out of the car, the hungry pack converged, encircling us.

Charlie handled it like a pro. Calm and composed while delivering a statement about false and defamatory claims, her unwavering commitment to victims, and her demand for a retraction.

Done.

You go, girl.

My sister doesn't weather storms. She is the storm.

Inside, I lock the door behind us in case a reporter gets bold.

Charlie wastes no time heading for her office. "I'll be a few minutes," she calls. "I need to speak with JJ and Garrett. And our lawyer. What a mess."

I exhale, my body sagging under the weight of everything we've just endured.

Five minutes. That's all I need. My noise-canceling headphones, a little deep breathing, and I'll be back in the game.

I make the turn into my office and—*whoa*. Jerome stands near my worktable, his long artist's fingers gliding over one of my brushes.

His honey blond hair falls in its normal shaggy waves around his ears, and my heart thumps.

Skidding to a halt, something inside me bursts. I've spent days avoiding him. Yes, there's been a fair amount of self-flagellation over it, but what I'm feeling now, the instant joy, the bone-deep missing, is...confusing.

How can I love him this much and still be afraid to marry him?

Ever-so-slowly, he angles away from the table and faces me. "Hi."

His tone is flat and...something. Something like sadness or disappointment. Panic slithers over my skin. My lack of attention, my total disregard for his mention of marriage, has done this to him.

I've done this to him.

I rush him. Just hurdle toward him, throwing myself into his arms.

Somehow, after how poorly I've treated him, he catches me. He even kisses the top of my head.

Resting my cheek against his chest, I breathe. Patchouli soap. Warm and earthy. So Jerome. He first tried it after we'd visited a farmer's market and hasn't stopped using it since.

He says, along with me, it settles him. We're his power combination.

Guilt once again thrashes me, and tears sting my eyes. I don't deserve him.

I truly don't.

We stay this way for what feels like a long time before I finally gather my courage to stand back and meet his gaze. Those hazel eyes? Seared into my brain. I could sketch them from memory.

"What are you doing here?" I ask.

"You wouldn't talk to me. I came to make sure you're okay."

"I'm so sorry."

"It's all right."

No. It isn't. "You're not letting me off the hook. You deserve better from me."

"Look—"

"Jerome—"

We both stop, then laugh.

And just like that, something shifts. We feel like us again.

But talking over each other won't get us anywhere.

He holds up his hand. "Me first. I know I ambushed you with the marriage talk."

"You didn't—"

He shakes his head. "Let me finish. Please."

I press my lips together and nod.

"We've never talked about marriage, and I could've been more thoughtful about how I brought it up. I get that it scares you, Meg. After the silence these past few days... I know I pushed you away. I'm sorry. I just..." He rubs the back of his neck. "Shit. I'm screwing this up."

"You're not," I say.

He pins me with another look, the heat so fierce it stirs that part of me that only Jerome can bring to life.

"I love you," he says. "And if you don't want marriage, that's fine. We'll keep things as they are."

A warm gush washes over me as relief takes hold. He's not dumping me. He's not forcing anything.

I'll admit, my immediate reaction is happiness. After all, I don't have to move out of my comfort zone. I don't have to do the thing that terrifies me.

Yay, me.

Except...I give his worn Pink Floyd T-shirt a tug. "Is that enough for you?"

He shrugs. "I don't know. For now, it is. I'm not sure what's tripping you up because, hell, Meg, we're practically living together, but...whatever. If you need time, take some time."

"I'm worried."

"About?"

I glance around the office, my attention skittering over the five skulls. Three complete and two in progress. Ariel, Martha, Nancy, Randy, and Peter. All cold cases. All names I've bestowed on them until we can identify them.

"I'm obsessed." I peer back at Jerome. "I don't know if I have room for all of them and being a wife."

He gives me a mock-horrified look that makes me laugh.

God, that laugh feels good.

Right.

I love this man.

"Meg, you are stone-cold nuts."

"And your point is?"

He snorts. "I could say the same about me. What do I know about being a husband? I'm a halfway-decent artist, part-time gallery clerk, part-time weed dealer, maybe-soon dispensary owner. I've never had a real relationship before you. At our age, that's... not great. But I love you. That's what I know." He shrugs. "The rest? I'll figure it out."

I cock my head, rolling his words around in my mind. We're a pair, aren't we? Both of us are thinking too much about what hasn't yet happened instead of focusing on right now. On being present and enjoying each other.

"You're right," I say. "I let my anxiety steamroll me. I'm so sorry. I should have talked to you. Told you that I was scared."

"Fear is normal. Shit. I'm scared every day when I open my front door. Anything can happen, right? I want it to happen with you. However, that needs to be. If you'll have me."

Always. Without question. "Absolutely," I say. "I love you, Jerome. I hope you know that."

"I do. But you can't ghost me again. I won't live that way."

Ooofff. That one lands hard. "I promise you, I will never do this again. If I freak out, I'll talk to you."

"Excellent. Hallelujah. Now we can both get on with it. Are we good?"

We are *so* good. "Sure are. I feel a thousand pounds lighter."

He bends low, brushing his lips against mine. "You make me insane."

I loop my arms around his neck. "I make me insane."

Then I full-on kiss him, pouring everything I have into it. My gratitude. My love. The last of my energy. He deserves that, even with everything else crashing down around me.

When we finally back away, I fan my face. "Phew. I've missed you."

At this, he smiles and lightly pinches my chin. "I've missed you. Now, I'm gonna get out of here. Let me know when you're available. Would love to see you."

I nod. "How about tonight at my place? It might be late. We

think we found a major clue. We have security footage of Mary Hartman taking something to the cottage."

"Whatever time works," he says. "I'll come by around eight. If you're not there, I'll wait."

Such a good man.

"Yes. I'd like that."

He drops a quick kiss on my lips and heads to the door. "Good. See you later."

I watch him go. His tall, lean frame moving away from me. "Jerome?"

He pauses near the door and swings back. "What?"

"You mentioned practically living together."

"And?"

"Maybe we can talk more about that. It's not marriage, but ... there's commitment there." I waggle my eyebrows. "We'll call it a trial run."

He grins at me. "Trial run. You're funny. Whenever you're ready, say the word and we'll talk."

Then he's gone, and just like that, I'm outside my comfort zone.

Maybe that's precisely where I need to be.

15

———————

Charlie

*T*he headline screams at me from my laptop: *"FBI Scandal: Forensic Psychologist Charlize Schock Accused of Misconduct."*

Breathe...

It's one of a dozen articles splashed across media outlets. I stare at the words until they blur, my fingers hovering over the keyboard as if I can delete them through sheer will. My Louboutins tap an anxious rhythm against the floor beneath my desk, matching my racing pulse.

"This can't be happening." I scroll through details supposed "inside sources" shared, alleging an affair with my former Bureau boss, Garrett Hastings.

I feel lightheaded. Dots dance at the corner of my vision. My fingers and toes tingle.

"Shit."

I'm nearing a panic attack.

Charlie Schock does not panic.

Ever.

Breathe, dammit.

The implications cascade through my mind like falling dominoes. My reputation. My credibility as an expert witness. My FBI consulting role. All of it—built from years of sacrifice— threatened by a lie.

Someone wants me off this case. Someone wants me ruined —someone like Mary.

My gaze drifts to the framed credentials on my wall—my doctorate and FBI commendations—symbols of a career I bled for.

I've fought too hard to get here. Too hard to let some tabloid-worthy fiction derail me.

I close my eyes again and grip the edge of my desk. *Inhale, exhale. You can handle this.*

"Charlie?" Meg's voice precedes her as she appears in my doorway. She looks brighter, steadier—like someone who slept for the first time in a week. "What are you going to do?"

I DRAW A FINAL DEEP BREATH. Release my death grip on the desk. "I'm going to do exactly what Mary doesn't want me to do." Tiffany's face flashes in my mind, clear as ever. I close the browser tab with a decisive click and open my case files.

The facts are what matter now, not some fabricated scandal. "I'm going to find who killed Tiffany."

"It's okay if you need to take a break to deal with this new wrinkle," Meg offers.

"When have you ever known me to back down from a fight?" I reach for my notepad and scribble a three-step action plan. Step one: prove Mary's dirty. The other two steps I'll play by ear once I do that.

My professional armor slides back into place. One panic

attack averted. "This is a distraction, nothing more, and I refuse to be distracted. Tiffany deserves justice, and I'm not about to let her down because someone is trying to smear my name."

Meg stares into her cup. "Have you talked to JJ?"

"Not yet. I take it things went okay with Jerome?"

A sly smile crosses her face. "Better than okay."

Another crisis averted. "You're not going to make me wear some god-awful maid of honor dress, are you?"

"The wedding is on hold for now. We're going to try an intermediate step—living together."

"Aren't you doing that already?"

"Not officially." Her grin is good to see. It softens the edges of my anxiety, if only for a moment. "Ready to get back to work?"

I close my laptop. "Whoever did this made their first big mistake. They've shown their hand—they're desperate."

I love the unwavering belief I see reflected in her eyes. "And desperate people make mistakes."

My phone rings, displaying a name that sends a complicated flutter through my stomach—JJ. I stare at it for two rings.

"I can see on your face that it's him," Meg says. "Take it. I'll be in the conference room with Mom when you're done. She's on a revenge rampage."

Oh Lord. I nod and accept the call. "Hey."

"Charlie." JJ's deep voice has a clipped edge. Cool. Contained. Disappointed...?

"Took you long enough to call." I maintain a neutral and professional tone. Despite our history, despite everything, JJ is still the U.S. Attorney, and I am a liability to him. Now more than ever.

"Are you okay?" The question comes out in a whoosh, genuine concern breaking through his professional veneer.

"I've been better." I absently caress the edge of my notepad with its action plan. "But I'm still standing."

His voice drops to that familiar baritone that can command attention in any room. "It's utter garbage. The lowest of the low."

No hesitation, no doubt in his tone. His voice is pure steel, the kind that melts anxiety on contact when it's directed at your enemies. One of the tightly coiled threads in my chest loosens. "It is. Garrett is a good friend, but we never—"

"Of course not. You're a professional above all else." *Like me.* He doesn't add those words, but they hover there, nevertheless.

"I know that, and you know that, but the rest of D.C. is having a field day."

"Listen to me." Rustling in the background. Pacing. Classic JJ when he's scheming. "This impacts both of us. Your reputation, obviously, but also the Hartman case, which means my office is in the middle of the tsunami. The timing is suspicious as hell."

"You think?" I can't help the sarcasm. "I know this puts you in a tough spot. *Again.* You can save the lecture. I'm truly sorry that it's affecting your office and Garrett. I wish I could shield you both."

"I didn't call to lecture you."

"You didn't?"

"What kind of cad do you think I am? I'm concerned about you."

"Oh." I can picture him perfectly—jaw set, those blue-gray eyes intense with that protective look that both comforts and irritates me. JJ always thinks he can fix everything.

"I want to make a statement," he announces. "Today. Go on record saying these allegations are baseless and politically motivated. I can affirm your professionalism, your integrity—"

Mom's not the only one on a revenge rampage. "JJ—"

"Hear me out." His voice slides into that jury seducing cadence. "You forget I've known you for ten years, Charlie. I can speak to your character. The Emperor of Cold Cases defending your honor will carry weight."

Something warm unfurls in my chest at his willingness to stick his neck out. He's willing to go public. To risk political fallout...for me. "That's appreciated, but I'm not letting you ruin your political capital. You've been positioning yourself for a Senate run for years. I won't let you throw that away."

His voice grows rougher. "Some things matter more than politics."

He's certainly had a change of heart. "Do they?" I'm not sure what I'm looking for, but maybe it's reassurance. "That's...true, but there's no need to panic." *I've got that covered.*

"Whatever is between us, this is wrong. Let me do this, Charlie. For once in your stubborn life, let me help you."

The offer is impulsive. Grand. Genuine. And utterly JJ. He never does anything halfway.

"I can fight my own battles," I say, softening my tone to take the sting out of the words. "But thank you. Truly. Right now, what I need most is for you to look at a new development in the case."

There's a long, awkward pause. His ego just got sideswiped. "And that is?"

"We spoke to the security guard on duty the night Tiffany died. He gave us a copy of the security camera footage—*untampered* footage. The version you sent me—yes, I know it was you—was altered to delete a scene where Mary left the house, went to the cottage, and ditched the purse before she called nine-one-one. We think the murder weapon may have been concealed inside it."

Dead silence. The knots in my chest start tangling again.. "I'll review it. But we keep this off the books for now."

Better than I'd hoped. "Tonight, my place. Say, eight?"

"Make sure no reporters are hanging around. We don't want to feed the sharks."

Chum. That's what I feel like right now. "I owe you."

"I expect payment in single malt scotch. The good stuff, not that mid-shelf crap you tried passing off the last time."

"Deal," I say, almost smiling despite everything. "See you tonight."

After we disconnect, I notice the flashing indicator of a waiting call on the landline. I buzz Haley. Her reply makes my stomach clench. It's Garrett Hastings.

The last person I want to talk to is the man I've been accused of having an affair with. But I owe him an explanation. "Garrett," I say. "Let me lead with, I'm sorry."

"Charlie." His voice is strained, little of his usual smooth confidence evident. "My phone's been ringing non-stop—the director, the Justice Department, every journalist from here to hell and back." He pauses, exhaling heavily. "Talk to me. What in the name of God just happened?"

Like me, his reputation and career are on the line, not to mention his thirty-some-year marriage. And I'm the grenade that just exploded in the middle of it.

I can't sit, so I jump to my feet and go to the window. Frost has gathered in the corners, and the view is not impressive, but if I crane my neck, I can see the front sidewalk. Now it's clean, but my life's a wreck.

Breathe. I stare at the framed credentials on the wall again, drawing strength from them. "Someone's trying very hard to discredit me, and they've dragged you into it." I give him a brief rundown on our investigation into Tiffany's case. He interrupts more than once to ask questions. To express disbelief. I refrain from telling him my theory regarding who's behind the attack.

Finally, he sighs. "Those with power and fame often believe they're above the law. You and I know differently. They attack us personally when they've got no other means of stopping us. We're not going to let them destroy your investigation—or your reputation. The work you and Meg are doing matters too much, and you have friends here at the Bureau." The sound of his door shutting and the squeak of his chair amplify his message. "I've got resources, databases, and enough balls to face this head-on. Whatever you need, it's yours. No strings attached."

That's the Garrett, I know—formal, fearless, and full of brass.

I press my fingers against the cool glass of the window, watching someone pass by on the sidewalk, now clear of reporters. Across the street, a few are still hanging out in vans, waiting for me to pop my head back out. Cars pass, and people go about their normal lives. Most have no idea of the chaos unfolding in mine. "I appreciate that, Garrett. More than you know."

"What's our next move?" he asks.

Our. The simple word reminds me that I'm not fighting this battle alone. Garrett and JJ are cut from the same cloth—honor, loyalty, fearlessness. Different styles. Same backbone. Both willing to help me. "We keep digging, but I have to be smarter about how I do it."

"You always did take challenges head-on."

Not subtle. It was a comment he put on one of my performance reviews. "And I've never been great at ignoring a dare."

"You know who leaked this false accusation to the media, don't you?"

I don't tend to make statements I can't back up with evidence. At least not to people like him. He always wants the facts, just like JJ. But hell, what's the worst that can happen at this point? "Tiffany's killer, Mary Hartman."

He gives a low whistle. "You have proof?"

"That she did this or that she's the killer? Neither, but I'm going to get it."

"I'm here if you need me." The sincerity in his voice is unmistakable. "Just say the word. But get this wrapped up. Fast. Please."

A flicker of doubt tries to take root. I snuff it out. After thanking him again, I end the call and gather a few tools of the trade and slip them into my coat pockets. A voice recorder. Pepper spray. A pen that's not just a pen.

Time to blow up a few things. "Mom," I call, walking briskly to the conference room.

My mother's head appears over her computer monitor, reading glasses perched on the end of her nose. "Are you okay?"

The question takes me off guard. Sometimes, she's still my mother, rather than an investigative journalist. Matt and Meg are at the table with her. They both seem to wait on the edge of a dime for my reply.

"Absolutely." I point at Mom. "I want everything you can find on Mary. Not the public profile stuff. I want financial records, connections to local businesses, and her ties to media outlets, especially those where she makes donations or has even the slightest whiff of financial interest. Anything she touches. I want to know where her fingerprints end, and someone else's begin. Matt, I want to know who she socializes with at the D.C. Police Department."

Mom's eyebrows shoot up, but she's already reaching for her notepad. "Give me a few hours," she says, waving me off. "I'll find what Mary doesn't want found. And I'll sharpen my teeth doing it."

My mother, the shark.

Matt's fingers fly over his keyboard. "On it, boss."

"Come on, Meg." I wave her to follow me. "We're going to grab lunch for everyone."

Meg frowns, her expression quizzical until she catches the nearly imperceptible jerk of my head. I know she gets it when the confusion in her eyes fades to clarity. "Right. Lunch. I'm starving."

"I could use a steak burrito from Juan's," Matt says without tearing his focus away from his screen. "If you're in that neighborhood."

Mom rolls her eyes. "Back in my day, we worked through lunch to get ahead of a story."

I slip on my coat with deliberate casualness. "We need fuel to fight battles. Besides, I can't think straight with my stomach growling."

Her eyes narrow. Years of journalistic instinct raise her suspicions, but she only nods. She's suspicious, but not enough to stop me. Yet. "Bring me back a sandwich—turkey on rye, no mayo."

"Will do," I say, already heading for the door.

Meg follows, matching my brisk pace. Neither of us speaks until we're safely in my car.

"We're not getting lunch, are we?" she asks.

A few reporters rush from their warm vehicles, waving microphones our way. I start the engine and honk for them to move as I pull out. "We might grab something on the way back. Right now, we're paying a visit to the Hartman estate."

"I knew it." Meg claps. "Mom will kill us if she finds out."

"Which is precisely why she doesn't need to know."

It takes a bit of finagling to get to the road, and we pick up several tails. Pesky reporters. "Seat belt," I remind Meg.

She shifts and buckles up as I begin some offensive moves learned while at the Bureau. Left, right, U-turn. If I had gone to the dark side, I could have driven getaway cars.

Once I'm sure I've lost the reporters, I mentally run through my action plan.

Meg interrupts my thoughts. "Don't you think Mary will refuse to see us?"

"I think she'll want to gloat about the damage she's caused." I check the GPS as it announces a traffic jam ahead and recalculates our route. "If she does, I'm going to get her on record." I pat my coat pocket where a listening device is ready to record anything the woman says. "Either way, showing up unannounced sends a message—I'm not backing down because of some tabloid shit piece."

"What did JJ say?"

"He offered his support."

Her eyes widen. "Finally. Now I don't have to kill him. And your old boss? Was he pissed?"

I change lanes. "He hid it well, but yes. He wants me to fix this, which means, solve the damn case and do it fast. But if I need his resources, I have them."

She squeezes my shoulder. "I'm proud of you."

I glance at her. "For what?"

"This type of attack hits you where you're vulnerable. You try to protect me, Matt, and everybody else, Mom and JJ included. This time, you couldn't. And your former boss? Mr. Hastings? I know how much you respect and admire him. To ruin his reputation and have him put before a firing squad because of you must be the worst kind of mortification."

If she only knew how true that is. "It's Special Agent in Charge Hastings, and yes, it's quite mortifying. But I can't sit back and let someone else control my narrative. I have no choice but to confront Mary and show the public it's all nonsense."

We fall into silence until we turn onto the tree-lined road that leads to the wealthiest enclave in the county. This is where money lives. This is where it buries secrets in the backyards. The houses grow more expansive, set back from the road behind ornate gates and manicured landscapes.

"Do you think we're crazy for doing this?" Meg asks.

"Probably."

"Well, then," Meg straightens in her seat as the GPS announces we're approaching our destination. "Let's go make Mom proud. Should I film it for TikTok?"

We both laugh.

The Hartman estate is a sprawling Georgian mansion with pristine white columns that stand out against the overcast sky. No reporters or Tiffany's mourners are present. Mary's been busy getting rid of them, no doubt.

"Subtle," Meg mutters, fidgeting with buttons on her wool jacket. "Nothing says 'we have nothing to hide' like a house that belongs in a Southern Gothic novel. How are we going to get in?"

The wrought iron gates part with mechanical precision, though I haven't announced our arrival into the security box.

Is someone expecting visitors?

Expecting *us*?

Mary.

Meg and I exchange a look. The driveway curves around an ornate fountain where water cascades over stone cherubs with vacant eyes. Even the angels look like they've seen too much.

Flowing water in winter. Impressive.

I park near the front entrance, mentally rehearsing the carefully crafted questions I've prepared on the way here. "We're here for a casual conversation. No accusations until it's time for them. We need to be smarter than Mary."

"We are smarter than that old bitch."

A smile breaks over my face. "I don't disagree."

My heels click on the herringbone brick pathway as we approach the imposing mahogany front doors. Two matching evergreen wreaths blot out the center windows. A miniature tree and red sleigh with fake presents decorate the porch.

"The decorations alone probably cost more than my annual salary," I whisper, noting the perfectly trimmed topiaries shaped like chess pieces flanking the entrance. Pawns and queens, all lined up for Mary's games. Even in the midst of winter, they're green and lush. I wonder if they're afraid Mary will yank them out by the roots if they show any weakness, like going dormant.

Meg nods. "I feel like I should've brought an offering."

"I'd rather bring a warrant." I press the doorbell. Seems redundant since whoever's home knows we're here. The resulting chime echoes deep within the mansion, a somber cathedral toll.

I expect a housekeeper or butler—someone paid to create distance between the Hartmans and unwanted guests. Instead, the door opens with unexpected swiftness, revealing a surprise.

"Charlie," Alex says my name as if he's happy to see me. His warm gaze shifts, and he spots Meg off to the side. "And Meg. What a pleasant surprise."

My carefully prepared opening line dissolves. He's barefoot in jeans and a Harvard sweatshirt—a casual appearance that contrasts with the formal setting and his typical appearance. His hair is slightly tousled, no hair products slicking it down today. He seems genuinely happy to see us.

"We were hoping to speak with your mother," I manage.

His smile flattens as he leans against the doorframe, blocking my view of the interior. "She's not here. It is the holidays. She has endless brunches, lunches, and fundraisers." He tilts his head. "Is there something I can help you with?"

Meg glances my way.

This wasn't the plan.

Abort, my instincts warn.

But my sister saves the day. "That's what I wanted to talk to her about—having a fundraiser for some cold cases we're working on. I have five skulls I'm rebuilding, and we have no identities for them yet. We're out of funds to keep pursuing our investigations into them, and you know how underfunded law enforcement is these days. Can we come in? Maybe run some ideas past you? Like you said, it's the holidays, a time for peace and forgiveness. We're waving the white flag. Finding justice for these victims will be a win for everyone. Your mother can rave to the media how the Hartman Foundation was instrumental in helping."

To my horror, Alex only hesitates a moment before he steps back, that winning smile returning. "I love that idea. We could call it"—he motions with his hand, creating an air marquee—"Reconstructing Hope. Or maybe, the Faces of the Forgotten Fundraiser."

Meg steps across the threshold.

When I don't, she glances over her shoulder at me.

"What are you doing?" I mouth.

My sister winks before she reaches for my arm and tugs me into the house.

16

Meg

There isn't an ounce of me that believes Alex is buying this Hartman Foundation nonsense. I see it in his eyes. That gleam. The hunger to know why we're really here.

Good for him. As nutty as this field trip is, I love the sheer ballsiness of it. We're solving this murder—no matter the cost.

Alex leads us into the foyer. Charlie gliding past him and pausing as he closes the door behind us.

The mansion is everything I expected, right down to the sweeping double staircase that curves up to the second floor. I love the symmetry it brings to the wide entry, but I'll never understand the waste of space.

Still, the designer opted for a minimalist style—creamy white walls and gleaming wainscoting.

A massive chandelier hangs from the vaulted ceiling. Sunlight streaming through the glass wall over the twin front doors makes the crystals glitter with flecks of azure, emerald, and rose.

The design is simple, but the scale—the sheer formidability—tells you everything this family wants the world to believe about their wealth, their power, their privilege.

Untouchable.

At least until now.

Alex gestures left. "Let's go in here."

He strides into the oversized living room, where an area rug that probably cost more than my duplex muffles the sound of our footsteps on the hardwood.

A Vermeer hangs over the white stone fireplace. An interesting choice, considering Vermeer specialized in quiet domestic scenes of middle-class life—something the Hartmans, with their obscene wealth, would never grasp.

I point. "Vermeer."

Alex gives a perfunctory nod. "My mother bought it at an auction. Not my favorite, but she likes it." He gestures to the sofa. "Please, have a seat. Can I get you anything? A drink?"

We both decline and settle onto the oversized white sofa perpendicular to the fireplace. Alex sinks into one of the giant armchairs across from us. Like the foyer, this room is built to impress—from the soaring ceilings to the enormous windows and the furniture that screams grandeur.

Mary Hartman is no fool. She understands all too well how to use her money to intimidate. It annoys the hell out of me, knowing it has shielded them from a murder investigation.

"So," Alex says, focusing on Charlie, "before you tell me more about this fundraiser idea, I have to say, I was appalled to see the headlines this morning. JJ's one of my closest friends. It's all rather shocking, no?"

Charlie, being Charlie, sits utterly composed, her face a bland mask, not a frown or raised brow in sight. "Clearly," she says, "someone's trying to destroy my reputation with this ridiculous accusation."

Alex gives her a well-practiced crooked smile. "Too bad it's not true. I'd have gotten to you before JJ."

Ew. So much for JJ being his *dear friend*.

My sister lets out a feigned chuckle. If it were real, it would light up her face with her electric, open-mouthed smile that could power this entire house.

Instead, she locks eyes with Alex. "I'm sure you've heard that JJ's out of the picture."

What the hell is she doing?

Flirting.

She's flirting to disarm him.

After holding her gaze a beat longer, Alex shifts his attention back to me. "If you like Vermeer, my mother has another in the dining room."

The dining room. If the floor plan in Mom's files was accurate, it's beside the kitchen, next to the door Mary walked out of in the security footage we watched this morning.

"Really?" I ask. "I'd love to see it."

"Of course." He points toward the hall. "Help yourself. Down there. Elena, our housekeeper, is in the kitchen—I'll buzz her to let her know you're coming."

Smarmy Alex is trying to ditch me so he can cozy up to Charlie.

Fine. I'll schmooze the housekeeper. See what I can find.

"Fantastic." I rise and glance at Charlie. "I'll be right back."

She offers a wave, fully understanding the plan. "Take your time. I'm sure Alex and I can entertain ourselves."

Blech.

I head down the hall, noting another classic I'd love to linger over, but...work to do.

I'll give Mary this much—she's got great taste in art.

The dining room is empty. Sure enough, a Vermeer hangs

on the far wall, but I don't have time to admire it. I move straight through the butler's pantry and into the kitchen.

Also empty. No housekeeper.

Hmmm.

Crazy Train—Mom's ringtone—blasts from my pocket. I check the screen where a text inquiring about lunch has popped up.

I ignore it, tuck it back in my pocket, and bring my attention to the kitchen.

Oversized windows overlook an expansive lawn. To the right sits the infamous cottage, its white paint gleaming in the sun like a beacon.

My phone rings again. Everybody Wants to Rule the World. Charlie's ringtone. I slide it from my back pocket and take the call.

"Hey."

"Hi." Her voice is so breathy, I nearly gag. "I've just been telling Alex I recently discovered the joy of ice hockey."

Ice hockey?

That'll be the day

"Oh-kay…"

I have no idea where this is going, but my sister is giving us an Emmy-worthy performance.

"Yes," she continues, "Alex has a signed Wayne Gretzky hockey stick. Can you imagine? It's in the trophy room in the basement. He's offered to show it to me."

The basement.

I glance out the window at the cottage. "By all means," I tell her. "Go. I'll enjoy the Vermeer a little longer. Meet you back in the parlor. Take your time."

Please. Take your time.

Translation: stall him. Make him think he's got a shot. Maybe he'll let the wrong body part do his thinking long enough for me to slip to the cottage.

If luck is on our side—not that it happens much—we'll be out of here before anyone monitoring the security video catches on.

I hang up. Seconds later, I hear Charlie's voice drifting from the hall, then Alex chimes in, their conversation fading as they move deeper into the house.

I glance back at the still-empty kitchen and slip out the back door, easing it shut behind me. The snick of the lock makes me flinch. If it auto-locks, I'm sunk. Checking it, I twist the knob easily and let out a relieved breath.

Then I sprint like hell toward the cottage.

Less than thirty seconds later, I duck around to the back, out of sight from the main house. There must be a back door.

I hope.

I slow, panting from the run. I really need to work on my cardio.

A door. Perfect. I jog over and test the handle. Locked. *Damn it.*

I step back, scanning. Six windows line the rear wall. I press my fingers against the glass of the first, push up. Nothing. Not even a wiggle.

I try the next. And the next.

My fingerprints are everywhere, but whatever. I have Charlie and Matt to clean up my mess from breaking and entering.

Third window. *Please, please—*

Unlocked.

I do my best, nudging the window up, my fingers sliding a couple times before I get enough of an opening to wedge my hand in and push it up.

I swing a leg over the sill and climb into a small bedroom with a full-sized bed and a dresser. A Rembrandt print hangs over the bed. Guess the cottage doesn't rate an original.

Keep moving.

I shut the window behind me and head into a short hall that opens into a modest kitchen and living area. I make quick work of checking the hall closet, behind towels, and under blankets.

No purse.

That would have been way too easy. Mary is more brilliant than that. I move into the master bedroom, foregoing the closet and looking under the bed. I attempt to lift the mattress, but—yow—my muscles buckle under the weight. Way too heavy.

I peer around the room, my eyes locking on an air vent. Too small. A Sherman would never fit behind there.

Living room. Maybe it's hidden in one of the chairs. I head that way. Just as I reach the end of the hallway, a knock sounds on the front door, and my insides curl.

"Hello?" a woman yells through the door. "Ms. Schock? Are you in there?"

Oh. Shit.

It must be Elena, the housekeeper.

"I saw you running," she continues. "Is everything all right?"

No. Not all right. Not at all.

The distinct sound of a key sliding into the lock scrapes against my nerves, and my pulse slams.

Shit, shit, shit. In a few seconds, I'll be face to face with the woman. I whip around, spot a door just off the kitchen.

The tunnel.

Alex told us about it connecting the cottage to the panic room under the main house. With no plan fully formed, I bolt for the door.

At the very least, maybe there's a lock and I can keep the woman out, while I decide my next move.

Charlie is going to kill me.

I swing the door open, revealing a small landing and a staircase. There's a light switch on the wall, but I don't dare flip it. I duck in just as the deadbolt disengages.

Glory be, there's a lock, so I flip it and draw a long breath. Focus, Meg.

"Ms. Schock?" the woman calls again.

As if I'd respond?

Still on the top landing, I slowly turn, holding the rail with both hands as I use my feet to feel my way down each step.

Step, step, step.

At this rate, it'll take me an hour to get to the bottom, but I can't risk the housekeeper seeing any light under the door.

As I make my way down, my brain locks on the idea that if someone hid a murder weapon, they wouldn't stash it in a closet where any guest could discover it.

Step, step, step.

No. They'd hide it where no one would think to look. I keep moving, slowly descending.

At the bottom, I drag my phone out and risk using the flashlight. This far down, it should be safe.

In front of me, a cement tunnel stretches out. Wise Meg begs me to go back and get out now, but who knows if the housekeeper is still up there. But I may never get this chance again.

And there's a murderer to catch.

I take off again, jogging the thirty yards to the door at the end that stands like a looming sentry.

Every nerve ending lights up like the Fourth of July. After all, someone might be on the other side.

When opportunity knocks...

Hands shaking, I grab the lever, press it down, and push the door open.

Motion sensors kick on the lights.

I glance around the door.

Empty room with cement walls painted a soft gray. A black

sofa is positioned against one wall, alongside a mahogany dining table and four chairs. On the far side, a door. I'm betting it leads into the main house's basement.

I swing my gaze left to a bunk bed with folded cots stacked between the frame and wall. Next to that is a four-tier metal shelf stocked with canned goods, a crockpot, and a toaster oven.

Panic room.

Has to be.

Holy hell.

I should turn back. I've been gone ten minutes already.

But I'm here.

I charge in and lift the sofa cushions. I find a bed and—a perfect hiding place—give the frame a good heave, opening it. Nothing.

I lift the mattress—nothing—then climb across it, checking the inside of the sofa.

Damn it.

The bunk bed is next. Same routine. Nothing.

I check behind every can, inside the crockpot, and the toaster oven.

I stand, scanning the room. What am I missing?

The table. I hustle over, eyeing the seam down the middle. Expandable. I grab an end and pull.

Hello.

Something in my chest kicks. It's like an all-out assault, and I let out a gasp.

Ohmygod. Ohmygod. Ohmygod.

In the compartment where the extra leaf should be sits a pristine black snakeskin purse.

A Sherman.

Ohmygod. Ohmygod. Ohmygod.

My phone blares again. Crazy Train.

I flinch so hard my neck locks.

I fumble for the device, jabbing it to silent just as the call goes to voicemail.

Before I can shove it away, a text from Mom pops in.

Where's my lunch? Are you okay?

I'm about to tap back a quick reply, just as a squeak from behind me sounds. Then I hear voices. Charlie's, getting louder as if trying to warn me.

I turn—slowly.

The door beside the sofa creaks open.

Run. It's all I can think. *Down the tunnel. Get out.*

Too late.

Alex steps into the doorway, Charlie's face peeking over his shoulder.

"What the hell?" he asks.

17

———

Charlie

*B*efore the muffled ringtone breaks the silence, I've gone down an uncomfortable rabbit hole with Alex. The basement lights cast a blue-white glow across his hockey memorabilia, giving the mounted jerseys and framed photographs an almost museum-like quality. He's slipped his feet into comfy loafers.

His shoulder brushes mine as he points to the signed Gretzky stick mounted behind glass over the fireplace mantel. "My pride and joy. Dad bought it for me when I was nine."

I could not be more bored, but I have to keep him preoccupied to give Meg time to check the cottage, so I smile and murmur just enough to keep him talking.

He moves onto a beat-up black puck encased in a glass box. "This one is from Ovechkin's rookie season." His voice drops to a reverent level. "Got it at an auction last year. Cost more than my first car."

I bite my tongue before asking if the car had a soul. I have no idea who Ovechkin is, and I have to keep the sarcasm out of my voice when discussing a puck being worth so much. "Wow." Feeble. I need at least fifteen more minutes. Can I buy Meg that much more time? "That's impressive."

Alex steps closer, his cologne—woodsy and expensive—filling the space between us. "Most women don't appreciate sports memorabilia. You know what they say about women who understand the value of a good slapshot."

I force a laugh, though I suspect there's a double entendre there. Something sexual? Probably. Ugh.

My mind switches tracks fast. The photos and layouts from Mom's boxes. Dimensions. Blood stains. Floor plans. Anything to keep me from rolling my eyes at his horrible pickup lines. "I'm no expert." Not about sports, anyway. Criminal minds? That's another story. "But I appreciate passion, and I can see that if I want to learn more about hockey, you're the guy to teach me." Bait, line, sinker.

The words hang in the air as Alex holds my gaze for far too long. "Passion is underrated. We could all use more of it, don't you think?"

Oh, boy. I smile and shift toward a collection of other pucks in glass cases. "And these? Tell me their stories."

He sidles up beside me, invading my personal space. I force my knees to lock so I don't step away from him. Act engaged. Meanwhile, I'm calculating square footage and trajectory angles. "They're all game-winners. That one's from the '98 Stanley Cup." His fingers graze mine as he points, the contact deliberate and lingering.

He launches into a story about acquiring the puck, and I chance another glance around the basement's wide-open space. The carpet must have been installed after Tiffany's murder. The police report mentioned bloodstains on the original flooring, but they've been covered up. Neat. Tidy. Like nothing ever happened.

The panic room door, nearly invisible against the back wall, is farther away than I'd expected from where I calculate her body landed. Photos can do that—mislead you, no matter how many, what angles, and how thorough the CSI techs were. Nothing beats standing in the room where the person died.

"What does that door lead to?" I ask, interrupting. "A bathroom?"

Alex huffs, unhappy with the change in subject. His gaze skates across the door, as if he can ignore it and it will disappear. He suspects I know exactly what's behind it. "That's the safe room." He settles on the couch arm, kicking his feet out and crossing them at the ankles. "Mom covered it for a while with a huge tapestry. The ugliest thing I've ever seen, but eventually, she took it down. She's lonely with Dad gone, and my sister and I out on our own. I visit every week, but the rest of the family rarely comes unless they need money or Mom orders us all home. Like she will for Christmas."

"We both have pushy mothers." I ease onto the edge of the couch cushion and wonder if I can get him to open the panic room. Probably not. Not without a scalpel or warrant. "It's nice to get to know you outside of work." I wave my hand at the hockey memorabilia. "Plus, getting to see this amazing collection is a bonus."

"You know what I think?" He slides off the arm and onto the couch next to me, causing the cushion to dip. "I think we have more in common than controversial mothers and a passion for hockey. I bet if we dig a bit deeper, we could find a few more common interests that would make for good dinner conversation, don't you?"

Dinner. *God help me.* The next words are out of my mouth before I can stop them. "Does that line typically work for you?"

"Yes." His smile shines with his ego. "But you're not typical, are you, Charlize?"

I tone down my instant reaction to cut him off at the knees. "I've been called many things, but 'typical' isn't one of them." I can't help it. I jump up and walk over to a framed photo of a younger Alex in a team uniform. "Tell me more about your own hockey career." Let's talk about something less dangerous, like teenage dreams and concussions.

He chuckles self-deprecatingly. "Not much to tell." As he talks about his junior traveling team and his dreams of being a hockey star, with pride evident in his voice, I continue to move about the room. Mostly, it's to keep space between us, but also to pinpoint where Tiffany fell.

When he takes a breath, I point at the panic room door. "Did your family ever need it?"

Alex remains rooted in place. He clears his throat. "No, thank goodness. I, uh, don't do well in confined spaces."

I turn, arching a brow. "You're claustrophobic?"

"Something like that."

"Sounds like you're correct about us having more in common. Mine is the result of an incident with Meg locking me in our mother's cedar chest when we were kids." A total fabrication. "No one found me for hours. You?"

Alex shrugs, attempting nonchalance. "Similar, but with that room when it was being built. There was no working panel on the inside yet. My cousin thought it would be funny to lock me inside. The shrink my mother dragged me to called it 'formative'—whatever that means." The word feels strained. Makes me wonder if the shrink had any idea what kind of man was forming. "All I know is I've avoided small spaces when possible."

Cousin? The panic room wasn't finished, so possibly the incident occurred before Tiffany was killed.

We know Tiffany taunted him by hiding his hockey stick in

there. That he'd asked Gordy to get it for him, suggesting he already had a fear of going in there. Had she humiliated him that night and then added insult to injury by taking his prized hockey stick and hiding it? Or had Alex suspected she was going to try and trap him, so he'd used Gordy to get the stick, then ended up stuck inside the room anyway? Had Tiffany poked fun at him, asking for Gordy's help, and Alex had then tried to prove he wasn't afraid of her?

His gaze drifts away from the door, a mixture of aversion and something else—shame, perhaps, or fear of vulnerability. Maybe guilt. The kind that doesn't disappear, even under new carpet. He notices me watching him and recovers quickly. "It's just a room."

That's when Crazy Train, the song I instantly recognize as the ringtone Meg gave Mom, sounds.

Alex's head snaps toward the door. "What was that?"

My pulse jumps. *What is she doing in there*? She's supposed to be checking the cottage for the Sherman purse. If she found something and used the tunnel...

Cottage.

Tunnel.

Oh hell.

I keep my voice steady despite the anxiety flooding my system. "Must be your housekeeper."

Alex frowns, moving toward the door with commanding steps that belie his earlier claims of avoiding the space. "That sound came from inside. Elena is supposed to be preparing my lunch."

My hand drifts to my pocket where my phone is, calculating how quickly I can call JJ if things go sideways. I type '*help*' and hit send. "Are you sure it came from in there?" I scan the area for a weapon. The fireplace poker is a contender.

When the security system beeps, Alex twists the handle and yanks open the door with unexpected force. The heavy metal swings wide, revealing slices of the room. I peer over his shoulder and hold my breath.

Shelves, furniture, artwork. No plants or homey touches. A sparse but functional space.

The view finally shows me what I feared—Meg.

She's frozen in front of a mahogany table, her phone clutched in her hand.

"What the hell?" Alex's voice cracks, his confident façade disintegrating into alarm, then fury. A vein pulses visibly at his temple, and his breathing quickens—the claustrophobia he'd mentioned earlier already wrestling with his growing anger.

I catch Meg's eye in a split-second of silent communication that only sisters who've spent a lifetime covering for each other can manage. Her wide-eyed look tells me everything. This wasn't her plan, but she's found something.

That's my sister.

"Oh! Meg, there you are." I infuse my voice with rehearsed surprise. "I was wondering where you'd wandered off to."

"How did you get in here?" Alex demands.

Meg brushes a strand of hair from her face. "I'm so sorry. I should have asked permission, but when I noticed the charming cottage at the back of the property, I wanted to take a look. I've just taken up painting, and the light bouncing off the frost gave me chills. I mean, total inspiration. I had to get closer and take a look. Once I was out there, I got snow in my boots, and I wandered inside to dry them out. Your mother has done such a beautiful job of decorating it." She's totally rambling. *Tone it down*, I think, but she barrels on. "The paint, the furniture—it's all marvelous. I hope you don't mind that I looked around. I stumbled across a door, and it led to a tunnel. And as Charlie can tell you, I can't resist a good tunnel. It harkens back to my Nancy Drew obsession."

"It's true," I add smoothly. "Meg gets caught up in textures and colors and loses herself."

Meg nods too enthusiastically. "Exactly! Even in here,"—she gestures at the room's walls and furnishings—"The mix of textures and design is fascinating."

Fascinating. Right. Because what else do you do when you stumble on evidence? *You compliment the furnishings.*

Alex crosses his arms. "Bullshit." He motions for her to exit the room.

Her posture stiffens. "Can you tell me about this piece?" she asks, hitching a thumb over her shoulder. "Midcentury, right?"

His jaw clenches. The Sherman purse—that damned monstrosity at the center of this whole mess—is partially visible in the well where the extra table leaf resides.

"I'll be damned." Alex's voice drops to a dangerous level. He grabs my arm and shoves me toward Meg. His grip is iron, his voice steel. "That's what this is about. Framing my mother for murder, isn't it?"

My heart hammers. This isn't going according to plan at all. It's a train jumping the tracks, and we're still on board. "That's not why we're here."

"Save it. You broke into my house to plant evidence. Jesus Christ."

What? That's not only wrong, it's dangerous. I tug my arm from his grip. "You invited us in, remember? And we're not trying to frame anyone."

"Then what do you call that?" Alex gestures at the purse. "Some kind of sick joke?"

"I found it there," Meg states. "And I haven't touched it."

"If your mother is innocent, then this might prove it," I say. "After all, why would it be hidden in the table? Work with us, Alex. If nothing is connecting Mary to the crime, we'll clear her name together."

Alex laughs, a brittle, humorless sound. "You two are just like your mother—obsessed with this, and destroying people's lives for your twisted entertainment."

A slap in the face. My mother's legacy always cuts deeper than it should.

"That's not fair," Meg interjects. "We're trying to find justice for Tiffany. You should be, too."

"At the expense of my mother?" Alex's voice echoes off the concrete walls.

Mother and son. A bond we've seen both of them honor above all others.

What if Mary is innocent?

What if Tiffany pushed one too many of Alex's buttons when they were kids and...?

I'm only a few feet from the table. "If the Sherman doesn't contain evidence against your mother, Meg and I will walk away." I meet his eyes.

"Let us examine the purse properly," Meg adds. "If there's nothing there, your mother is cleared. If there is..." She lets the sentence hang.

Alex's jaw works, the muscles in his neck standing out like cords. "I've had enough. I'm calling the police." He pulls his phone from his pocket, fingers trembling as he jabs at the screen.

This isn't the righteous anger of a son defending his mother —this is the desperate panic of someone with everything to lose.

"Go ahead," I tell him. "Call them. I'm sure they'd be very interested in examining that purse, too. Probably with a forensics team."

He hesitates, his thumb hovering. He lifts his gaze to me, and the basement suddenly feels twenty degrees colder.

Meg and I are facing down Tiffany's killer.

"You're not worried about your mother at all." I force Meg behind me as I take another step closer to the purse. "You're worried about yourself. You're not protecting *her*. You're trying to save *you*."

Meg gasps, understanding dawning on her. She pinches my arm. Hard. Sending me a message.

Alex's voice is as hard as her pinch. "I don't like what you're implying."

Too late to turn back now. "I'm not *implying* anything. I'm stating a fact." Meg pinches me again, a warning. I keep talking. "Tell us how it happened. Did Tiffany start with the hockey stick and then lock you in here? When you got out, were you so traumatized that you went after her? The photographs of the body's position show it facing away from the door, suggesting she was walking away from this room. Possibly running."

His eyes widen fractionally—just enough for me.

I see it play out in my mind. "You snapped. You jumped her, grabbed the first thing you could reach, and held her down while you beat her with it."

Meg peers around me to ogle him. I'm hoping she has her phone recording all of this. "Oh, Alex. Is that true?"

"You're insane." But his hand holding the phone drops to his side. "Both of you. I never touched that girl."

That girl. Signifying a mental and emotional distance he's put in place.

"Prove us wrong," I challenge. "Let the police examine everything. Let's settle this once and for all."

His gaze darts to the half-exposed purse. I recognize the moment fear supersedes logic. His mask slips farther. Panic wins. He springs forward with shocking speed, driving his shoulder into my sternum. The impact sends me crashing against Meg, who yelps as we slam to the ground.

"Stop!" I yell.

"Charlie!" Meg pushes me off her. "Get the purse!"

Alex is already at the table, snatching up the Sherman and clutching it against his chest like it contains his very survival. It bulges, and I'm certain we've found the murder weapon.

I get to my feet. "Give me the purse, Alex."

He turns for the exit. I grab the back of his shirt.

He twists away, strong-arming me and sending me crashing into the table. "You're not ruining my life!"

Meg jets forward to block his escape. "This isn't helping your case, Alex. If you're innocent—"

"Innocent?" He gives a strangled laugh, his eyes wild as he stalks toward Meg and the exit she's barring. His claustrophobia is creating panic. "You don't know anything. You don't understand what's at stake. Get out of my way!"

He tries to shove Meg aside. She grabs his arm, and they spin awkwardly, knocking into a display case. She grunts but doesn't let go.

"The claustrophobia isn't real," I yell at him, grabbing for the purse. "It's guilt closing in on you!"

A primal sound tears from his throat. He dances away. Meg jumps up, out of breath. "Charlie, I've got—"

Alex's elbow connects with her chin, sending her stumbling into a sofa. She somersaults over it.

I grip his collar, pinning him against the wall. His eyes are unfocused, his pupils dilated with fear.

"Can't breathe," he gasps, clawing at my hands. "Can't—"

The former hockey player knows how to deliver a body check. His knee drives upward, missing my groin but catching my thigh. Hard.

I falter, losing my grip. He shoves me, sending me into a shelving unit. The unit collapses under me, biting into my spine. Glass shatters. Pain slices across my neck and hands. My ankle twists painfully.

Meg screams my name. She starts toward me, then veers, reaching for him instead as he dashes for the door.

He swings the purse in an arc, catching her in the temple. She falls.

And doesn't get up.

I push up from the broken display. Blood warms the silk of

my blouse. I must have bitten my lip, too. The taste of copper fills my mouth. My ankle throbs. "You can't escape this, Alex. JJ knows. He's on his way."

The panic drains from his face, replaced by ice-cold hate. The dread of what comes next, what we've uncovered, burns away his claustrophobia, leaving only adrenaline.

He backs out of the room, the purse still clutched to his chest. Before I can give chase with my wobbly ankle, the door slams shut with the finality of a tomb.

And, of course, we don't know the code.

18

Meg

Pain explodes at my temple, and I hit the floor hard. My head's spinning like one of those tilt-a-whirl rides I used to love at the county fair and my vision is fuzzy. A handbag didn't do that—it was whatever was inside it.

Flat on my back, I blink up at the ceiling. It has a weird fuzziness to it, so I blink a few more times, trying to clear the fog.

"Meg!"

Charlie's voice cuts through the haze with her classic get-'er-done sharpness I've heard my entire life. Even as a child, my sister was bossy.

"Don't yell," I croak, pushing myself to a sitting position while a blast of pain ricochets through my skull.

Charlie looms over me, blood staining her mouth and clothing.

"Are you okay?" I ask.

"I'm fine. Bit my lip. The rest are cuts from the glass. Alex is getting away. Can you get up?"

He's getting away. With the purse?

Foggy brain or not, I launch to my feet. Stomach tumbling and head pounding, I bolt for the main house's door.

"Locked."

I turn back, sidestepping Charlie. "This way. We can go through the tunnel."

"We'll never catch him."

"We have to try."

I yank open the tunnel door and take off, every step like a pickaxe to my battered head. My stomach lurches again. If I'd eaten anything, I'd be vomiting.

"This tunnel," I call over my shoulder, not bothering to check if Charlie is with me. I know she is, "leads to the cottage. From there, we can cut across the lawn and hopefully catch him before he escapes."

At the end of the passageway, we bolt up the stairs. Charlie is right on my heels now, her longer legs able to cover more ground even within the confines of her tight skirt. At the top, I step aside and point to the front door. "Go. You're faster."

She kicks off her shoes, hitches up her skirt, and blasts through the door without a concern over running through snow barefoot.

That's Charlie—zero concern for comfort and all in on justice.

By the time I reach the porch, she's already ten yards ahead, tearing toward Alex's car in the circular drive. Her left ankle wobbles a few times, but it barely slows her down.

I zero in on the house, where the front door opens.

Alex. Purse in hand.

"There he is!" I yell. "Take the back of his car. I've got the front!"

We branch off. Alex tracks us but keeps moving and jumps into the driver's seat.

Charlie veers to cut him off at the lower driveway. I barrel forward, ready to throw myself on the hood of his car if necessary.

I want that purse.

Alex hits the gas and speeds down the long path. The gate is already opening and — dammit, dammit, dammit—he's getting away.

I push myself, picking up speed.

To my right, Charlie shifts slightly, moving toward the tiny gatehouse.

If she's hoping to get the gate closed before Alex screams through, she'll need a miracle.

A black SUV slides into view, blocking the exit.

Alex brakes hard. Tires screech. The high-pitched squeal nearly gives me a brain bleed, but I keep moving, trying to level off my breathing that's coming in short bursts.

The SUV's door flies open and...what the hell?

JJ.

Of all the people who shouldn't be here right now, it's probably him.

"Don't let him leave!" Charlie shouts, still barefoot and fierce.

The sight of JJ spikes my adrenaline as I close the last twenty yards.

"What the hell is going on?" JJ thunders as Charlie comes to a stop beside him.

Alex pops out of his car, taking cover behind the door. "Step aside, JJ. I'm leaving."

"Not until I get some answers."

"He has the purse!" I shout. "Don't let him leave!"

I reach the passenger door and grab the handle. Locked.

The Sherman is right there on the seat.

I jab at the glass. "There's something inside that purse. He just clocked me with it."

I glare across the hood at Alex. "And it hurt, you son of a bitch."

"JJ," Alex says, his voice courtroom calm. "They've lost their minds. They came here uninvited, and Meg did an illegal search of the property."

JJ eyes me.

"He's not wrong," I say. "Well, except the part about us losing our minds. He's definitely wrong about that. And he hit me! I found the Sherman hidden in a table. I didn't touch it, but I know there's something inside it. He hit me with it and my head is freaking killing me!"

The knock of a motor—I'd recognize that sound anywhere—draws my gaze to the gate where my van pulls in behind JJ's SUV.

Oh no.

The driver's door opens. Mom hops out like she's storming Normandy. She plants her feet, lifts her arms, and points a gun.

My mother.

With a gun.

JJ showing up is one thing, but Mom? I can't wait to hear how this all came to be.

"Mom!" Charlie barks with that same sharpness she used on me. "What are you doing?"

"I took one of your guns from your safe."

"I see that," Charlie mutters. "Someone remind me to change the code."

"Helen," JJ says, his voice dropping to an I-will-destroy-you level, "put that gun down before you hurt yourself. Or I swear to God, I'll have you locked up on a list of gun charges the length of my arm."

Poor JJ. No escaping the Schock madness.

All eyes but mine swing to her. I'm fixed on Alex. I dart

behind the car. JJ has the front blocked, and unless Alex runs me over, he can't go backward.

He's trapped.

And now?

We get answers.

19

Charlie

JJ strides toward Alex's car with easy confidence. His breath forms small clouds in the frigid air, one hand raised in a lazy salute. A man walking into a poker game rather than a showdown with a killer.

I stand frozen at the gate, my fingers gripping the cold metal. They've gone numb, though I'm not sure if it's from the cold or the tension coiling inside me.

My feet burn from the snow. My ankle sends white-hot pain up my leg.

"Seems like there's been some misunderstanding," JJ says, his voice unconcerned. He glances at me as if confirming Meg's story. I give a nod. His gaze slides down my legs to my stocking feet, and a small crease forms between his brows. "Why don't we go inside, and everyone can give me their version?"

Yes, please. I'm turning blue.

Meg's hands go to her waist. She doesn't seem dizzy, so

that's a good sign. Between her head injury and my frostbite, we'll need a tour of the ER soon.

Mom hovers like a mother lion near JJ, my gun at her side. I see the anger in her expression, and I second it—I want to throttle Alex myself for leading us on this chase. For hurting Meg. I ease closer to Mom, intent on relieving her of my weapon.

God. My mother has my gun and is ready to shoot this man.

Alex's hand tightens on his car door. "I was just leaving."

"Won't take long," JJ says. His tall frame casually blocks Alex from running, just like his car blocks the end of the grand drive, a chess move so smooth Alex probably doesn't even realize he's been cornered. "Grab the purse, and let's go inside."

My heart beats hard against my ribs. A brutal chill racks my body. I watch Alex's eyes dart to the Sherman bag sitting on his passenger seat. "It's my mother's," he replies, as if this explains everything.

It does.

JJ nods. "Mind if I take a look?" I hold my breath, watching this masterful performance. JJ, the Emperor of Cold Cases, is playing the part of friend to perfection. Charming. Casual. Not Alex's boss. Not the man who's going to call the police and have him arrested.

Alex hesitates, and a flash of something dark crosses his face—calculation, fear, desperation—before he composes himself again. He's spooked.

"Actually," JJ continues, his tone light, "why don't you take it out and show me? The craftsmanship on those things is supposed to be exceptional. At least, that's what Charlie tells me. She's into that designer stuff." His gaze flicks to me again, to my feet. "I wouldn't know a Sherman from a knockoff."

A standoff ensues, brief but sharp as static. Alex's eyes flick around, mind racing for an escape that doesn't exist. He knows

—knows—that JJ is playing him, but he's too polite, or too cornered, to admit it.

With a drawn-out reluctance, he reaches across the seat and retrieves the bag. "Fine." He places it on the hood of his car. "It's just a purse. I don't know why Charlie and Meg are making such a big deal out of it."

But it isn't just a purse. It's the linchpin.

It's a loaded gun in a designer disguise.

As it sits there between them, Alex drums his fingers against his thigh. His eyes dart between JJ, the Sherman, and the street beyond.

"How much is a vintage purse like this worth?" JJ asks, not touching it yet, just admiring it from where he stands.

Mom shifts, tired of the game. Meg is coiled like a spring.

Alex hedges. Behind his eyes, I see a recalculation. His composure is melting like the snow under my feet.

"My mother is innocent," he blurts, his voice rising with an edge of agitation that splits the air. "She didn't kill Tiffany. I don't care what you think that purse proves."

JJ maintains that perfect poker face. "I never said anything about murder."

Alex blusters. "That's what this is about. That's why the sisters came here." His gaze sweeps past JJ to pin me. "Look, I took it because it belonged to my mother. That's all. When your sister tried to stop me, I panicked."

The lie is clumsy, but it gives him something to hold onto. I walk alongside JJ's car. Out of the corner of my eye, I notice a blanket on the backseat. "So, you hit her with it? An overreaction, don't you think?"

"It was an accident," he insists. "A misunderstanding." He jabs a thumb toward Meg. "She's a menace, just like your mother. I didn't mean to hurt her, but I have limits, you know."

JJ nods, his expression so neutral it could win medals. "Why run if it was just a misunderstanding?"

"Because I knew how it would look!" Alex's desperation is palpable now. "Everyone's been trying to pin this on my family for years. I have to protect them. Always have."

"I need to get Charlie off this snow," JJ says, doing a one-eighty. He motions at me and his car. "Why don't you hop inside?"

Not that he doesn't care about me and my feet, but this is a stall tactic. To keep Alex guessing. Keep him off guard. JJ walks back to his car and opens the door for me. Alex's eyes dart around frantically, this gaze lingering on the Sherman, then shifting to the street.

I've seen the same look on cornered suspects just before they make a desperate move.

JJ bends down to dig into his glove box. He pulls out evidence gloves and a polyethylene bag that he folds and places inside his coat pocket. There's a Beretta next to all of it. "Be ready," he mutters.

I lower my voice as I slide onto the cold seat. "I don't think he's armed. If he were, he would've used it already."

Alex goes for the purse, snatching it with clumsy desperation. He nearly drops it before clutching it to his chest and bolting down the driveway past us.

JJ starts to go after him but slips on the ice. I bail out and shout, "Come back here, you bastard!"

Meg is moving, too, a blur on my right. "I've got him!"

She veers left to avoid colliding with Mom, her chunky winter boots giving her traction that my wet, stocking feet can't match. My sister, usually lost in her artistic world of reconstructing faces, moves with surprising athleticism.

I do a wobbly flail and slide. Mom catches me, and both of us almost go down. "Alex, stop!" I shout, more to distract him than anything else. "You're only making it worse!"

He hits the road and glances back, fear twisting his face.

That split second of distraction costs him.

His slick loafers hit a patch of dirty snow, and he stumbles.

That's all Meg needs. She hurls herself forward in a tackle so solid that it would make any NFL coach proud. They crash to the ground with a spectacular thud, snow exploding around them in a powdery cloud. One of Alex's shoes flies off.

"You bastard!" Meg shouts, punching him repeatedly in the back and shoulders. "Now I get it. All this time, we were chasing the wrong Hartman. You killed Tiffany."

JJ marches past me and Mom. I catch up, my feet numb.

Alex's face is pressed into the snow, one arm pinned awkwardly beneath him, the other still desperately clutching the bag. Meg's face is flushed with exertion and victory. Her years of hauling clay and plaster have given her upper body strength, easy to forget until now.

"Alexander Hartman!" My mother's voice cuts through the air. "I wouldn't move another muscle if I were you."

My head snaps around to see Mom striding to us, handgun pointed directly at Alex.

"For God's sake, Mom!" I hiss. "Meg is right there."

JJ pushes me toward her. "Take care of that. Now."

Alex freezes, terror and disbelief mixing in his expression as he stares at the barrel of the gun. The weapon looks absurdly steady in Mom's hands, like she's practiced this moment in front of a mirror for years.

Has she?

I position myself between her and Alex, my hand outstretched. "Give that to me before you end up back in jail, this time for murder."

For a tense moment, she doesn't move. I see that familiar gleam in her eyes—the one that appeared whenever she thought she was onto something big. Then, with a resigned sigh that fogs in front of her face, she flips the safety on and places the gun in my palm.

"You always were too sensible," she says with disappointment.

Yep, that's me.

Behind us, Meg is still punching Alex. "Meg," JJ commands. Just her name.

I shove the gun into my waistband and grab my sister's shoulders. She's shaking with rage. "Meg, stop." I pull her off him. In the distance, sirens pierce the air.

She struggles against my grip, her eyes wild. "He bashed her head in and left her there!"

"I know," I say as JJ rips the Sherman from Alex's grip and slams a foot down on his back to keep him pinned. "I know. But we're not like him. We get justice the right way."

Meg's breathing is ragged. Her body vibrates, but she stops fighting me. Her shoulders drop a fraction, her jaw unclenches. "The right way," she repeats, almost to herself. She looks down at Alex, who's visibly shaking on the pavement. "Fine."

"Let's see what was worth all this trouble," JJ suggests, opening the bag.

I hold my breath, feeling Meg do the same. Mom draws closer, eager.

JJ reaches in, and when his gloved hand emerges, he's carefully holding the very end of a hammer. Not just any hammer —a claw hammer with a wooden handle, its metal head gleaming dully in the winter light. There's something dark crusted along one edge.

Meg's voice is a strangled whisper. "Oh my God."

"Probably blood." JJ slips it into the evidence bag so as not to destroy fingerprints. "And what appears to be hair."

"Tiffany's murder weapon." The words feel surreal as they leave my mouth.

The sirens draw closer. I retrieve a second, larger bag for the purse. Mom smiles.

"You two," JJ says, looking at Meg and me, "are either the

most determined or the most reckless women I've ever met." The corner of his mouth twitches upward. "Probably both."

"Family trait," Mom chimes in.

I laugh—a sharp, sudden sound that surprises even me.

JJ grabs Alex by his collar and hauls him back into the driveway, slamming him against the side of his SUV. Alex's face crumples.

The cockiness is gone, replaced by something small. "That's not—" he starts, then stops. His eyes dart between all of us, and I note a slight twitch at the corner of his left eye. The way his hands keep opening and closing. His shallow breathing. "You don't understand."

"We're going to have this conversation at the station." JJ's tone brooks no argument.

Alex reaches for one last desperate attempt at control. "You won't believe me anyway."

Meg, still breathing hard from the chase and tackle, straightens her spine. "We don't have to," she says. "Evidence speaks louder than words."

I climb into the back of the SUV to get my poor feet off the ground. "That's the thing about forensics, Alex. Blood doesn't lie."

Mom hails the police units that pull up at the curb and then lights up when she spots a news van. As uniformed officers approach, I grab the blanket and wrap myself in it. Closure is rare. This moment—watching Alex being read his rights, the evidence bags containing the hammer and purse being carefully documented and secured—feels surreal.

Meg climbs in beside me and rubs my arms. "How bad are your feet?"

"I'll live. How's the head?"

"Hard as granite." She knocks her fist against it. "I'll live."

We share a grin. JJ approaches as Alex is placed in the back of the cruiser. "Are you two out of your ever-lovin' minds?"

"The Emperor of Cold Cases delivers again," I say, attempting to divert his anger.

He shakes his head. "This was all you. Both of you."

Mom is giving a speech to the reporter who waves a microphone in her face.

"And her," I say, nodding in Mom's direction. "She's the one who insisted we take it on."

"Tiffany can rest easy this Christmas," Meg says.

JJ starts the vehicle and turns up the heat. I groan as it rolls over me. Meg agrees to walk him and one of the officers through the house, tunnel, and cottage to explain what happened. I lay down on the seat with my blanket and drift off.

Later, someone pulls on my toes to wake me. I shoot up to find JJ peering at me from the open door. He hands me my shoes, purse, and coat. "Time to give your statement." An officer hovers behind him. "Then I'm taking you to the hospital."

I yawn and wiggle my toes. They ache, but they all work. I cram my feet into my pumps, grimacing. "No hospital. Statement, and then I'm going home. I need a vacation."

Meg has left with Mom. After I've given the officer my account of what happened, I head for my car.

JJ stops me. "One of the officers will drive it to your place." He nudges me back into his SUV. "I'm driving you home. We need to talk."

20

Meg

"Here's one," Jerome says from his spot beside me on his battered sofa. "Two bedrooms. Decent neighborhood."

It's Christmas Eve, and we're enjoying some quiet time together before my family's big holiday feast tomorrow. Typically, I look forward to Christmas Day, but this year—with all the energy spent on solving Tiffany's case, Mom's drama, and Charlie heartbroken over JJ— I'm not sure what I have left in the tank.

Being an empath, I suck up every ounce of my family's energy. And, right now, the energy isn't good.

At all.

So, yes, I'm savoring my time on Jerome's couch.

We're killing time before we watch the original A Christmas Carol. I love that movie. It gives me a sense of the simplicity before technology hijacked everything.

171

While we wait, Jerome is scouring real estate rental websites. He's been at this for days and has come up with zilch.

Well, that's not altogether true. He's found options I've nixed for at least a dozen reasons. Too small, too loud, too isolated.

He holds his phone up. Onscreen is a photo of a brick apartment building. Brick? And no porch. No outdoor fireplace to curl up beside on a fall night.

Nooooo.

I shift my gaze from the screen to him. "I know you've been working hard on this, and I keep saying no."

"You do," he says, the words carrying zero heat. "I know it has to be the right setup."

Between us, we need at least one art studio. Thus, a two-bedroom. Even then, we'd need storage space for supplies and any extra items we bring from our own homes.

We need space. And what he's finding in our price range doesn't provide that.

"I have an idea," I say. "I know we said we wanted to start fresh somewhere. A place we could make our own."

"I hear a 'but' coming."

I grin and playfully tweak his nose. "So smart!"

He snorts, and we share a laugh that makes me thankful, once again, I have this man in my life.

I almost let him go. All because I'm terrified of losing him.

Ironic, is all I can think.

"What if," I say, "you moved into my duplex? The mortgage payment is manageable, and the house is bigger than anything you've looked at. The art studio is already set up, and there's still a third bedroom. I know it's next door to Charlie, but she's not a problem. We already respect the boundaries. If your car —or JJ's—is in the driveway, we don't bother each other."

Jerome shrugs. "I've been thinking about that. We've been living in our places for so long that I didn't anticipate how expensive it would be to start over. But what if, and I'm not saying it'll happen, living together doesn't work out? I don't want to ruin—emotionally speaking—your place for you."

Jerome. Always so thoughtful. I love that about him.

I lean in and kiss him softly, lingering for a few seconds while my body comes to life. We've been making up for lost time in the bedroom the last two days, and clearly, I'm not done.

Before my hormones derail this conversation, I back away. "I love you," I say. "Thank you for thinking ahead and looking at all the angles. No matter what happens with us, I'll always love you. Always. If we don't work out, I'd still have a home with a bunch of great memories."

He holds the phone up again. "It would keep us from dealing with this search."

"You'd be free of the dreaded rental apps."

At this, he smiles. "Thank God. It's your place, Meg. If you're comfortable with it, I say let's try it."

Relief, that glorious loosening of muscles, flows over me. I've hated the idea of leaving my house but understood Jerome's point. He wanted something that was ours, not mine. After his rental hunt, he doesn't seem all that bothered by us staying in my place.

It makes so much more sense.

Out of the corner of my eye, I catch a flash of red on the television screen. Breaking news. The anchors are suddenly onscreen. I grab the remote and unmute the volume as Felicia, the lead anchor, begins speaking.

"Alex Hartman, son of local philanthropist Mary Hartman, has been charged with the murder of his cousin, Tiffany. The case has stumped law enforcement for thirty years, and now a local cold case group has helped solve this crime. Let's go live to Abigail Gaines outside the Hartman mansion, where Citizens Solving Cold Cases is holding a vigil."

Oh boy. My mother must be loving this.

The screen cuts to a young brunette reporter, presumably Abigail. The camera pans wide and—

Yep.

There's my mother.

Two hours ago, she was at the grocery store stocking up on everything she needed for tomorrow's meal.

"Isn't she supposed to be at home with your dad?" Jerome asks.

I hold up a hand and focus on the screen. Mom is wrapped in the coat Charlie gave her for her birthday last year. Perched on her head is a black hat expertly positioned so her hair falls across her forehead.

My mother may be insane, but she knows how to work a camera.

"My father must be losing it. And there goes our fantastic homemade meal."

I scoop my phone from the coffee table and text Charlie: *PUT THE NEWS ON! NOW!*

"Good evening," Abigail says. "I'm here with Helen Schock, president of Citizens Solving Cold Cases." She angles to face Mom. "Helen, thank you for joining us. What can you tell us about why you all are out here."

"Well, Abbie," Mom begins, her voice thick with concern, "on the anniversary of Tiffany's death, where else would we be? That child was brutally murdered in this home. A time when all children should feel safe and loved."

I groan. "She's really laying it on."

"Finally," Mom says, "after years of law enforcement dragging their heels and pandering to the Hartmans, we have an arrest."

"Oh. My. God," I say, my voice rising because what in the actual hell is she doing?

Charlie is already on the outs with JJ. This stunt will infuriate him.

It's bad enough that the U.S. Attorney's office, JJ's office, is in disarray after his deputy was arrested. JJ already blames us for interfering in his case, and now Charlie is forced to spend Christmas without him while our mother antagonizes the situation.

I turn to Jerome. "I may have to kill my mother."

"You've said that before."

"Let's hope," Mom continues onscreen, "with all the work done by CSCC and Schock Investigations, that we'll finally, finally, get justice for this poor child."

"If she says 'finally' one more time," I say, "I'm absolutely killing her. JJ will make sure I don't get convicted."

My phone alerts with an incoming text. Charlie. I mute the television and check the text. A stream of creative profanity fills the screen.

"Yikes," I say. "Charlie isn't happy."

"Can you blame her?"

"Not in the least. JJ is already fending off media inquiries and doing damage control while the press is screaming about how a murderer was on his staff for years and nobody noticed."

Jerome peels back his lips. "Not a good look. Is the case solid? I mean, is there a chance Alex will get away with it?"

"JJ won't tell us anything, but Mom heard from her source at the police department that Alex confessed."

Jerome's eyebrows shoot up. "Really?"

I nod. "Apparently, Alex, Tiffany, and a few other kids were playing in the basement. Tiffany thought it would be funny to lock him in the panic room. Have I mentioned Alex is claustrophobic?"

"Ouch."

"Right. She left him in there for a good ten minutes. When his mother started looking for him, Tiffany ran back down to let him out. By then, he was having a full-blown anxiety attack. When she opened the door, he lost it. Total rage. There was construction happening in the basement. He grabbed a hammer and struck her from behind."

"Jesus. They were kids!"

"It's horrific. He freaked and ran to get his mother. That's when the Hartman machine went into action. These people are evil. She told him to get the Sherman purse, and then she hid the hammer in it."

"Wait," he says. "Didn't you tell me there was security footage of Mary taking the bag out the back door to the cottage? Why didn't she use the tunnel?"

"It wasn't connected yet. At that time, the only way to the cottage was above ground. She hid the purse there until the police were done in the main house. At some point, she took it back to the panic room when she knew the house wouldn't be searched again. According to Alex's confession, his mother was too paranoid to get rid of the murder weapon. Being the control freak she is, she didn't want to risk dumping the hammer and someone finding it. She felt the safest place would be in the panic room. Where she knew it would be safe."

"Alex gave all this up? Totally implicated Mommy dearest?"

"According to mom's source, he did. He claims he didn't need to tamper with any evidence while he's been at the US Attorney's office, but he fed his mother information about Charlie for her smear campaign. Now, Mary is facing a slew of charges. Evidence tampering, accessory after the fact, obstruction..."

Jerome lets out a whistle. "Merry freaking Christmas."

How I love him.

"If Alex did confess, and there's no reason to doubt it, he and Mary will spend most, if not the rest, of their lives in prison."

"The family name," he says, "was more important than that little girl. I can't wrap my mind around that."

"I'm telling you, evil."

The image on the television shifts to A Christmas Carol, already in progress.

"Well," Jerome says, settling back into the cushions, "guess we should plan on bringing food tomorrow. Your mom is obviously not cooking."

Contemplating this, I curl into Jerome's side, wondering where, at such late notice, I can get a fully prepped Christmas meal.

21

Charlie

Thanks to Meg and Jerome, Mom's dining room table groans under the weight of steaming dishes of rosemary potatoes, a glistening ham, and colorful salads. Mom has added her signature sweet rolls, which smell like childhood Christmases at this same table. And me? I brought wine.

Dad's laugh is infectious. Mom gestures wildly as she tells her version of how she nailed Alex. Yes, it was all her if you buy this story. Meg and Jerome argue good-naturedly about the Nationals' prospects.

I smile and nod at the right moments, but all I can think about is JJ's face when he dropped me off at my house--his no-holds-barred speech and his parting words.

"Charlie?" Mom's voice breaks through my thoughts. "Would you like more wine?"

Damn straight I do. But I have to be sober enough to drive home. Still, I push my glass forward, wondering if the second glass might dull the ache in my chest. Meg refills my water, giving me a concerned look. Or is it pity?

Dad eagle-eyes me. "You okay, kiddo? You've been quiet tonight."

"Just tired," I lie, taking a sip. It's not really a lie. I am tired. Tired of the emotions that have left me wrung out and brittle.

What I can't say is that I keep replaying the last conversation I had with JJ in my head. "You'd think he'd ease up on being right all the time," I mutter under my breath, stabbing a potato.

"What was that?" Mom asks.

"Nothing. These potatoes are amazing."

Meg clears her throat. Jerome's honey-blond hair is pulled back in a neater-than-usual low bun, and he's upgraded from his typical grunge clothes to preppy. The sight of him looking so conventional is cute, and I'm happy about Meg's decision to live with him.

He gives Meg's hand a quick squeeze. "Hey, Charlie," he says, sliding a dish my way. "Want to try my famous seven-layer dip?"

"By 'famous' he means he once won third place at a neighborhood cookout," Meg stage-whispers, making everyone laugh.

"It was second place," Jerome corrects with mock indignation.

I watch them, envying that easy comfort between two people who understand each other. The ache in my chest intensifies.

My sister catches my eye as I politely take a scoop of the dip. "We agreed—no cold cases this weekend. Don't tell me you're working tonight, of all nights."

I shake my head. "Just admiring Jerome's transformation. Did you dress him, or did he manage that sweater all by himself?"

"Hey!" Jerome protests good-naturedly, although Meg gives me a warning glance. She can't decide if I'm teasing or being snarky. I'm not sure, either. "I'll have you know I picked this out without any assistance," Jerome says.

"And it only took him three tries," Meg adds, as she serves herself some fruit salad.

A timer goes off in the kitchen, and Mom jumps to her feet. "The pie!"

She rushes out and Dad joins her. "Don't burn yourself," he calls to her.

Meg leans forward. "Seriously, are you okay? You've got that thousand-yard stare you get when you're profiling people."

I wave her off and take another sip of wine. "It's nothing."

"Uh-huh. And this has nothing to do with a certain tall, dark, and lawyerly man whose name rhymes with 'Hey-Hey'?"

I nearly choke on my wine. "How many gummies have you had today?"

She rolls her eyes. Jerome chuckles. "I can vouch that she only had the recommended dose to get through this dinner."

It's my turn to roll my eyes, although it's actually a smart move. "Did you bring any brownies?"

"That bad, huh?" Jerome asks, knowing that I never indulge.

Meg points her fork at me. "Come on, spill. What happened with Mr. Perfect Suit?"

I push food around on my plate. "Nothing. It's fine."

"Your face doesn't say 'fine.' It says, 'I'm pretending to be at this dinner while mentally rehearsing conversations with a man who isn't here.'"

I toy with my glass. "Look at me—totally present and enjoying this lovely family dinner. See? No problems here."

Meg mercifully drops the subject as Mom and Dad return, the pie safely cooling and not burned—an unusual state of affairs.

Mom asks Jerome about his latest art commission, and I

exhale slowly, grateful for the reprieve. I take another bite of ham, tasting nothing. All I can think about is whether JJ is eating Christmas dinner alone. Nothing but leftovers and a legal pad.

Meg kicks me under the table.

"...and then the anchor asked me about my determination to solve Tiffany's case." Mom's voice rises with excitement as she gestures with her fork, nearly sending a piece of glazed carrot flying. "I told him it was my duty. Inspiring the cold case group is my passion. You should've seen his face when I broke down the psychological profile I developed on Alex Hartman."

She developed? Huh.

Her eyes snap with the same intensity they had when Meg and I were kids, watching her hunched over newspaper clippings at the kitchen table. Except now, the entire family is her captive audience as she recounts her moment in the spotlight. "The producer says they're considering having me back as a recurring expert," she continues. "Only a few months at the Crime Desk, and I'm getting the recognition I deserve."

Dad squeezes her hand. "You're brilliant, honey. I recorded it. Twice, actually, because I thought the first one might not have caught everything."

"It wouldn't have happened without you girls, of course." Mom glances between Meg and me. "I made sure to mention you, you know."

"For about fifteen seconds," Meg whispers, but her smile remains genuine.

Dad forks up some ham. "What matters is that everyone is safe. When I think about what could have happened..." His voice cracks. "I don't care how good the story is—nothing's worth losing any of you."

Mom nods. "Absolutely right."

I manage a smile. The case is closed, the danger past, my family safe. All the boxes of a happy ending are neatly checked.

So why do I feel like I'm watching the celebration through a pane of glass, unable to truly connect with the joy around me?

Mom segues into talking about the makeup artist and cameraman, how they finally got her good side. Dad hangs on every word, pride radiating from him. Jerome and Meg exchange knowing glances, amused by Mom's dramatic story-telling.

Mom raises her glass. "To justice and good journalism."

"And to family," Dad adds.

I lift my glass mechanically. "To family," I echo, wondering if anyone else can hear how hollow the words sound.

Mom scrutinizes my plate. "Charlie, you've barely touched your dinner."

The potatoes have gone cold. Most everyone else is done and ready for pie. I seize the opportunity, setting my napkin beside my plate. "I need to call it a night." I stand and smooth my skirt. "Dinner was lovely. Thank you." I lean down to kiss Dad's cheek, then Mom's. "Merry Christmas."

Meg rises and envelops me in a hug. "Call me," she whispers fiercely in my ear.

"I will," I promise, knowing she'll be banging on my door before the night's over.

Matt calls me on the way home. "Merry Christmas. Thanks for the bonus. Thought the coffers were empty."

I'm at a stoplight and use it to keep from looking directly at his mug on the screen. The dip into my 401(k) came with a hefty fee. The six pairs of designer shoes I sold online have left a big hole in my closet. Still worth it. "Santa rewards the faithful."

He snorts. In the background, Taylor waves at me over his shoulder. "Hey, Charlie. Merry Christmas."

Their place is festooned from top to bottom with lights, garland, and a pile of discarded wrapping paper near a giant spruce. "Merry Christmas."

"I have a present for you," Matt says.

The light changes, and traffic begins to move. "That's sweet, but I don't need anything."

"We're not leaving D.C." Taylor leans down so her face is next to his. "I've been offered a position here that's even better than Atlanta."

"You're staying?"

Matt gives me that knock-out smile of his. "Thought you were getting rid of me, didn't you?"

A weight lifts off my chest. "Congratulations, Taylor."

She shrugs immodestly. "Garrett Hastings reached out. He's forming a new task force, and my skills fit."

My former boss. I didn't call in his favor to help resolve Tiffany's case, but he's on the mayor's new federal review team. Now, SAC Hastings has helped me in a whole other way. I'd better order him a gift basket. "He's tough but a stand-up guy. You'll like him."

"I'll be in tomorrow," Matt says. "Try to stay out of the news until then, okay?"

I give him a half-hearted smile. "No promises."

MY HALF of the duplex greets me with blessed silence, a stark contrast to the symphony of voices and clattering dishes I left behind. I slip off my heels at the door, my feet sinking into the plush area rug as I flick on the entryway light.

"I was beginning to think you weren't coming home."

My heart catapults. JJ lounges in the dimness of my living room, illuminated only by the streetlights filtering through the blinds. He's in a charcoal Tom Ford suit that fits his expression, his eyes watching me with an intensity that makes my skin prickle.

"Breaking and entering is a federal offense, Counselor," I manage, though my voice betrays me.

He rises, all six-foot-four of him unfolding with his usual effortless grace, but under it is a level of sheer exhaustion. "I still have a key."

He does. Damn. "Abuse of power. Add it to the list."

A ghost of a smile plays at the corner of his mouth. "I brought wine." He gestures toward my kitchen counter, where an open bottle of cabernet breathes beside two glasses. "And an apology."

I don't move, trying to reconcile the rush of conflicting emotions—the anger that's been simmering for days, the relief at seeing him, the apprehension about what comes next. "You could have called."

"You wouldn't have answered."

His certainty stings only because it's true. Maybe. I'm not sure at this point. "You don't know that."

"I know you."

Smartass. He does know me. I move to the kitchen, needing distance, needing something to do with my hands. JJ remains where he is, giving me space. "Family dinner?" he asks.

"Where else would I be?" I pour myself a glass of the wine, not offering him one. "Although it was more Mom's celebration of her media triumph. She got seven minutes on the morning news to discuss how she cracked the case."

"And how many of those minutes acknowledged your contribution?"

I take a long sip. "It doesn't matter."

He grins, loosening his tie with one hand. The familiar gesture sends an unwelcome ripple through me. "For what it's worth, I gave you and Meg all the credit at my press conference."

He watches my reaction to see if I already know. If I watched it.

I did. "I don't need credit." I stare into the wine glass. "I just need—" I stop myself. What do I need? Respect? Understanding?

"How are your feet?" he asks, changing topics.

I curl my toes when he glances at them. "No permanent damage, but still super sensitive to cold." Even now, I'm dying to ditch the stockings and pull on my warm, fuzzy socks. In previous days, I would let him warm my feet. His foot massages are legendary.

"Another battle wound for Charlize Schock's collection." His attempt at lightheartedness falls flat.

Silence stretches.

"Charlie." My name comes out soft on his lips. "I should have done things differently with this case. I made a mistake. You and Meg—"

"Don't." I set down the glass with too much force. Wine sloshes over the rim.

He steps close enough that I can smell his cologne. "I've spent the last three days trying to figure out how to right this very off-course ship."

The directness of his statement catches me off guard. JJ doesn't admit to being wrong. He prosecutes, he persuades, he wins.

"You didn't trust my judgment." The words burn my throat. "But you did your job. I don't blame you for it."

"I shouldn't have put my job above you. Us. I..." He shakes his head. "My heart is wreaking havoc on my head."

"Maybe that's the problem. You're so used to being the smartest person in the room you can't imagine being wrong." I hold up a hand before he can retort. "Again, you were between a rock and a hard place. I get it. You're a professional. You did what you needed to. I just wish..." What? That he would have defied his boss and the mayor and still chosen to work with me over their direct orders? *Wow, Charlie. Great job of standing in your power and still wanting him.*

A sharp exhale leaves his mouth. "I'm not good at this."

Neither am I. "Which part?"

"The part where I admit I've met my match." A hint of his usual confidence returns, tempered with something new. "The part where I acknowledge that I need a partner who understands my job, my position, and doesn't bail when we hit rough waters."

What's with all the sailing metaphors?

My buried anger blasts through me. "You bailed on me." I jam a finger into his chest. "I'm calling you on your bullshit. I didn't give up on us. *You* did. And just because I understand the predicament you were in, I don't forgive you for it."

He takes another step closer, his height making him impossible to ignore in my small kitchen. "You see? That right there. You don't let me hide behind my title or my reputation. I need you, Charlie."

He's too tall. Too broad. Too...everything. I have to get away. "Tough." I swipe my wine as I brush past him. My heart breaks as I say, "You blew it."

He follows, leaving careful space between us as I plop onto the couch. "I'm used to controlling situations. You know that. My whole career is built on anticipating what comes next. But with you..." He sheds his jacket and throws it on the recliner, pacing in front of the coffee table. "You test me. You take risks that make my blood run cold. You put yourself in danger all the damn time."

"And you calculate every risk before taking a single step."

He stops, studies me. I expect an argument. Instead, I get the opposite. "Maybe we balance each other."

The simplicity of his observation makes me laugh. "I'm not going to stop being who I am. And I happen to analyze every option to achieve my goal. You make me sound like I'm a wildcard when I'm anything but. I know people. I study them. How they act and react. I'm damn good at what I do."

"You are." He crosses his arms and rubs his chin. "This isn't really about our different styles or the demands my job places on me that can cause us problems, is it?"

"There's no more *us*, JJ. You made that choice, so stop overthinking it."

"If I quit my job, would you reconsider?"

I choke. "What?"

He sinks down next to me on the sofa. Not touching me, but close enough that he could. "I don't want a future that doesn't include you. If I change jobs to one that doesn't put us at odds with each other, would you at least give me a second chance?"

I hop up, once again needing space. My living room is bare of any holiday decorations. Not a smidge. It's sad, really. I'm so consumed by work, I don't take time to appreciate the passing years.

My pulse is trippy, my heart hammering. I want to say yes, but in the end, I know if he quit being the U.S. Attorney for the District of Columbia, he'd only end up resenting me over it. He loves his job as much as I love mine. We're not normal. With our jobs. With seeing justice done. With giving a voice to those who don't have one. To those, like Tiffany, who've been silenced.

I'm now the one pacing. "Do *not* quit your job. That would be the stupidest thing you could ever do."

"You terrify me, Charlie. You know that, right?"

I stop cold. "I *terrify* you?"

"You're the most fearless person I know."

My heart flutters. Stupid thing. "Not fearless. Determined." I gesture between us. "But this isn't a case you can solve with your charm and legal brilliance. This is...messy."

"I like messy." The corner of his mouth lifts in that smile that first caught my attention years ago when he was still a married man. I'd fallen head over heels for him. "And I like you. Your bullheadedness. Your guts. Your astute mind." His gaze drops seductively to my feet. "And your toes."

My heart stutters. My toes press into the carpet. "You're not smooth-talking me into taking you back."

At first, he says nothing. He just watches me, like he's afraid to blink. Then, he stands, and even though he doesn't move, the space between us feels smaller. "This isn't flattery to get you back into my bed. I'm serious. I don't want easy, Charlie. I want real. And you're the most real thing in my life. We've had conflicts before, and we've overcome them. We'll no doubt encounter them again in the future. You have every reason not to trust me now, but I'm telling you, I'll do whatever I need to to gain that trust back."

Including quitting his job.

I can't imagine him doing anything else. He was born to be a prosecutor. A leader.

I search for any hint of the practiced charm he uses in courtrooms and press conferences. Instead, I find only JJ—confident but exposed, waiting for my verdict.

"I just..." I swallow my fear. "I can't go through this again. I don't give my heart to just anyone, you know." My voice breaks. "You were it for me."

I see the restraint it takes for him not to move. Not to come to me and sweep me into his arms. "You're the only one for me, too." Now, he does move. Only to step around the end of the table. When I back up, he stops. "I was an ass. I failed you."

"You did." It would be so easy—too easy—to forgive him. I force myself to stand my ground. No dodging. No avoiding. I take a purposeful step toward him. "I still respect and admire you, but I don't think you can earn back my trust."

He hangs his head. "Will you at least let me try?"

I truly realized my love for JJ was too big, too overwhelming, when I saw him shot right in front of me several months ago. When his blood covered my hands.

When I knew I couldn't save him.

This abyss between us... Can I save him this time? Can I save us both?

All it takes is one word. One impossible but straightforward word that's stuck in my throat.

Yes.

As if he senses this, he hands me my wine glass. I down the contents in two gulps, wipe my lips with the back of my hand.

Even with the liquid courage, I can't say it.

Yes.

I can't say no, either.

He nods, a defeated movement, grabbing his jacket and pulling it on. "Okay. I'll let you be." He strides for the door, shoulders slumped. There, he turns, holding onto the knob, the cold winter air rushing in. He scans me one more time. "Merry Christmas, Charlize."

And then he's gone.

I glance around at the furniture. My lack of decorations. The emptiness of it all.

Meg is moving into a new phase of life. Mom, too. But me? I'm still stuck where I've always been. Tenacious, ambitious, successful. But happy? Fulfilled? Satisfied?

I was when JJ and I were on the same page. We had a future.

A future he threw away, I remind myself.

But Charlie Schock goes after what she wants.

And she gets it.

Nothing in my life worth a damn has been easy. I don't do easy.

I do messy.

And then, I organize it. Analyze it. Profile it.

Love is a psychological necessity. It's as essential to our well-being as food and water. Romantic love fulfills a basic need. Plenty of studies have shown that couples, for all of their faults, are stronger together than their individual parts. Passion and intimacy are only two parts of love. Commitment is the third.

It wasn't simply trust that JJ had broken. It was that commitment.

If he was willing to quit his job to be with me, he was still committed. His lapse had been temporary.

Didn't mean I forgave him.

But...

A host of swear words fly out of my mouth. I grip the bowl of the wine glass so hard that I might shatter it. I set it down. Rushing to the door, I throw it open.

He's already in his SUV. He looks up. Turns off the ignition. Steps out.

I stand on the porch, shoeless, toes rebelling. "We're not done. I have more to say."

A grin teases the corner of his mouth. "Are you going to say it out here and risk frostbite?"

I glance at my feet. My toes are burning. Not freezing. Their sensitivity to the cold feels like I'm sticking them in fire. "Do you want to come inside? I have a rare Macallan you might enjoy."

"You bought me a present?"

"You said I owed you. This is me balancing the ledger."

JJ reaches for me then, and I step into his embrace without hesitation. His arms envelope me completely, and I press my face against the solid warmth of his chest. For the first time in days, the knot in my stomach unravels.

"I've missed this," I whisper against the soft fabric of his coat.

His arms tighten around me, and he lifts me off the ground. "I've missed you."

He carries me inside, using his foot to close the door. We stay in our embrace for a long moment, as if making up for all the ones we've recently spent apart. His heartbeat thrums steady and strong beneath my ear.

"I'm sorry I shut you out." He pulls back just enough to look down at me. "Never again."

"I put you in a terrible predicament, but you should have talked to me. Tried to work something out."

He brushes a strand of hair from my face. The tenderness of the gesture nearly undoes me. "I was trying to protect both of us. It didn't work. But I'm pretty persistent when I want something, and I want this, Charlie. Us."

"Even though I'm stubborn and complicated and messy?"

"Because you're stubborn and complicated and messy." He leans down until his forehead rests against mine. "And brilliant and brave and exactly who I want to be with. You make everything harder. But also, better. That's love, right?"

The words settle my pulse. Fill the hollowness in my chest. When his lips meet mine, I welcome it. There's a lot of work to do to mend our relationship, but I don't want anyone else.

We end up on my couch with the wine and whiskey, fingers intertwined, talking about everything and nothing. The case, the media circus, Mom's television appearance.

"So, what happens next?" I ask, watching his thumb trace circles on the back of my hand.

He muses over the last sip of his drink. "Dinner tomorrow? Somewhere without dead bodies or your mother?"

I laugh, the sound surprising me. "That narrows it down in this city."

"I know a place," he says. "And after that, we figure it out day by day."

Day by day. Not rushing ahead or planning every move. Just taking things as they come. "No quitting your job. Not yet," I insist. "I may need you to help me with future cases. You know, using my feminine wiles on you."

He laughs. "I'm looking forward to you trying that."

When I start yawning, he washes our glasses, dries his hands, and heads for the door.

"Thank you for waiting for me tonight," I say. "For not giving up."

A quirk of his mouth. A kiss that lingers before he says, "You're worth waiting for."

After one last kiss, I let him out, close the door, and lean against it. Will things work out? I don't know, but it's Christmas. Miracles happen, right?

A knock startles me. I open back up, thinking it's JJ.

It's Meg. She points toward the street "Was that...?"

I grin. "It was."

"Things are okay?"

"Mostly."

"But he's not playing Santa and coming down your chimney tonight?"

I quirk a brow. "We're taking things slow."

Jerome is hauling a stack of gifts out of his vehicle and lugging them to her place. "Night, Charlie," he calls.

I wave. "Goodnight."

Meg hugs me. "I'm happy for you. But if JJ so much as looks at you wrong..."

"I know. You'll kick his ass."

She winks and goes next door to be with her partner.

I'm alone. The place feels too big, now that JJ's gone. I grab my phone and text him.

Wanna play Santa? Come down my chimney? My toes are cold. Really cold.

There's a brief pause. He probably just hit the highway. Then: *We can't have that. Get in bed. I'll be there shortly.*

I smile to myself while I strip off my clothes. I climb under the covers. When he appears at the bedroom door a few minutes later, I hold out my arms. "Ho, ho, ho," I say, relieved when his clothes hit the floor and he joins me under the blankets. "Merry Christmas to me."

"To us," he corrects.

And then he warms all of me.

THANK YOU FROM THE AUTHORS

*H*ello!

Thank you for reading this book. We hope you enjoyed it! If you did, please help others find it by leaving a review at Goodreads or your favorite retailer. Even a few sentences about what you loved about the book will be extremely appreciated!!

Thank you!

Misty & Adrienne

MEET ADRIENNE

 Adrienne Giordano is a *USA Today* best-selling author of over forty romantic suspense, mystery and women's fiction novels. She is a certified life coach with a passion for helping people reach their goals. Adrienne is a Jersey girl at heart, but now lives in the Midwest with her ultimate supporter of a husband, sports-obsessed son and Elliot, a snuggle-happy rescue. Having grown up near the ocean, Adrienne enjoys paddleboarding, a nice float in a kayak and lounging on the beach with a good book. For more information on Adrienne's books, please visit www.AdrienneGiordano.com. Adrienne can also be found on Facebook (AdrienneGiordanoAuthor), Instagram and Goodreads.

Don't miss a new release! Sign up for Adrienne's new release newsletter!

BOOKS BY ADRIENNE GIORDANO

PRIVATE PROTECTORS ROMANTIC SUSPENSE SERIES

Risking Trust

Man Law

Negotiating Point

A Just Deception

Relentless Pursuit

Opposing Forces

THE LUCIE RIZZO MYSTERY SERIES

Dog Collar Crime

Knocked Off

Limbo (novella)

Boosted

Whacked

Cooked

Incognito

The Lucie Rizzo Mystery Series Box Set 1

The Lucie Rizzo Mystery Series Box Set 2

The Lucie Rizzo Mystery Series Box Set 3

THE ROSE TRUDEAU MYSTERY SERIES

Into The Fire

STAND-ALONE ROMANTIC SUSPENSE BOOKS

Crossing Lines

Deadly Odds

HARLEQUIN INTRIGUES

The Prosecutor

The Defender

The Marshal

The Detective

The Rebel

JUSTIFIABLE CAUSE ROMANTIC SUSPENSE SERIES

The Chase

The Evasion

The Capture

WOMEN'S FICTION

BY ADRIENNE WRITING AS ANNE DANO

The Money Shot

JUSTICE ROMANTIC SUSPENSE SERIES w/MISTY EVANS

Stealing Justice

Cheating Justice

Holiday Justice

Exposing Justice

Undercover Justice

Protecting Justice

Missing Justice

Defending Justice

SCHOCK SISTERS MYSTERY SERIES w/MISTY EVANS

1st Shock

2nd Strike

3rd Tango

4th Silence

STEELE RIDGE ROMANTIC SUSPENSE SERIES w/KELSEY BROWNING

& TRACEY DEVLYN

Steele Ridge: The Beginning

Going Hard (Kelsey Browning)

Living Fast (Adrienne Giordano)

Loving Deep (Tracey Devlyn)

Breaking Free (Adrienne Giordano)

Roaming Wild (Tracey Devlyn)

Stripping Bare (Kelsey Browning)

Enduring Love (Browning, Devlyn, Giordano)

Vowing Love (Adrienne Giordano)

STEELE RIDGE SERIES: The Kingstons w/KELSEY BROWNING

& TRACEY DEVLYN

Craving HEAT (Adrienne Giordano)

Tasting FIRE (Kelsey Browning)

Searing NEED (Tracey Devlyn)

Striking EDGE (Kelsey Browning)

Burning ACHE (Adrienne Giordano)

STEELE RIDGE SERIES: The Blackwells w/

TRACEY DEVLYN

Flash Point, Book 1 (Tracey Devlyn)

Smoke Screen, Book 2 (Adrienne Giordano)

Cross Roads, Book 3 (Tracey Devlyn)

Crash Course, Book 4 (Adrienne Giordano)

End Game (Tracey Devlyn)

MEET MISTY

USA TODAY Bestselling Author Misty Evans is celebrating her 100th published novel in 2025. She loves writing urban fantasy, paranormal romance, and mystery/suspense. Under her pen name, Nyx Halliwell, she also writes supernatural cozy mysteries.

When not reading or writing (which is most of the time), she enjoys music, movies, and hanging out with her husband, twin sons, and three spoiled rescue dogs. She's a crafter at heart and has far too many projects to finish.

Visit www.mistyevansbooks.com to check out her online store and sign up for her newsletter.

BOOKS BY MISTY EVANS

Don't want to miss a single release? Sign up for my newsletter at www.mistyevansbooks.com

Black Swan Division Romantic Thriller Series

Redeeming Meg

Tempting Tessa

Avenging Jessie

SEALs of Shadow Force Series

Fatal Truth

Fatal Honor

Fatal Courage

Fatal Love

Fatal Vision

Fatal Thrill

Risk

Listen to the series on the Eleven Reader Publishing App!

SEALS of Shadow Force Series: Spy Division

Man Hunt

Man Killer

Man Down

Covert Affairs

Operation Ambush

Operation Contraband

Operation Sleeping With the Enemy

Operation Heist

The Justice Team Series (with Adrienne Giordano)

Stealing Justice

Cheating Justice

Holiday Justice

Exposing Justice

Undercover Justice

Protecting Justice

Missing Justice

Defending Justice

Schock Sisters Mystery Series w/Adrienne Giordano

1st Shock

2nd Strike

3rd Tango

4th Silence

The Secret Ingredient Culinary Mystery Series

The Secret Ingredient, A Culinary Romantic Mystery with Bonus Recipes

The Secret Life of Cranberry Sauce, A Secret Ingredient Holiday Novella

The Accidental Reaper Series, available in ebook, print, and audio

Grim & Bare It, Book 1

Reaper's Keepers, Book 2

In Too Reap, Book 3

Killin' It (short story for newsletter subscribers only)

The Vampire's Kiss (an exclusive short story available in Misty's Store.
Intended for mature audiences 17+)

Grave Girl

Grave Magic

Grim Vows

Undead Ever After

Listen to the series on the Eleven Reader Publishing App!

The Kali Sweet Series, available in ebook and print, and audio.

Revenge Is Sweet, Kali Sweet Series, Book 1

Sweet Chaos, Kali Sweet Series, Book 2

Sweet Soldier, Kali Sweet Series, Book 3

Sweet Curse, Kali Sweet Series, Book 4

Sweet Malice, Kali Sweet Series, Book 5

Sweet Betrayal, Kali Sweet Series, Book 6 (coming winter of 2025)

Listen to the series on the Eleven Reader Publishing App!

Witches Anonymous Step 1

Jingle Hells, WA Step 2

Wicked Souls, WA Step 3

Dark Moon Lilith, Witches Anonymous Step 4

Dancing With the Devil, Witches Anonymous Step 5

Devil's Due, Witches Anonymous Step 6

Dirty Deeds, Witches Anonymous Step 7

Wicked Wedding, Witches Anonymous Step 8

Listen to the series on the Eleven Reader Publishing App!

Soul Survivor, Moon Water Series, Book 1

Soul Protector, Moon Water Series, Book 2

Listen to the series on the Eleven Reader Publishing App!

COZY MYSTERIES (WRITING AS NYX HALLIWELL)

Sister Witches Of Raven Falls Mystery Series

Of Potions and Portents

Of Curses and Charms

Of Stars and Spells

Of Spirits and Superstition

Confessions of a Closet Medium Series

Pumpkins & Poltergeists

Magic & Mistletoe

Hearts & Haunts

Vows & Vengeance

Cupcakes & Corpses

Tea Leaves & Troubled Spirits

Haunted Honeymoon

Wedding Bells & Psychic Spells

Phantoms Are Forever

Skeletons & Scandals

Cooking With Ghosts: Hauntingly Good Southern Recipes

Murder & Marigolds (Coming Spring 2026)

Listen to the series on the Eleven Reader Publishing App!

Sister Witches of Story Cove Series

Cinder

Belle

Snow

Ruby

Zelle

Sister Witches of Story Cove Complete Set

***

Witchy Candy Shop Mysteries

Tricks and Treats

Candy and Creeps

Gum and Ghouls

www.ingramcontent.com/pod-product-compliance
Lightning Source LLC
Chambersburg PA
CBHW071301190726
48292CB00007B/2633